THIS FEELING FOR YOU

A Town Called
Forgotten

BOOKS BY RACHEL BRANTON

Lily's House Series
House Without Lies
Tell Me No Lies
Hearts Never Lie
Your Eyes Don't Lie
Broken Lies
No Secrets or Lies
Cowboys Can't Lie

Finding Home Series
Take Me Home
All That I Love
Then I Found You

A Town Called Forgotten
Kiss at Midnight
This Feeling for You
Reason to Breathe
Everything About You
Never Letting Go

Other
How Far
Royal Quest

Picture Books
I Don't Want To Eat Bugs
I Don't Want to Have Hot
Toes

UNDER THE NAME TEYLA BRANTON

Unbounded Series
The Change
The Cure
Protectors
 Ava's Revenge
 Mortal Brother
 Set Ablaze
The Escape
The Reckoning
Lethal Engagement
The Takeover
The Avowed

Other
Times Nine

Imprints Series
First Touch (prequel)
Touch of Rain
On The Hunt
Upstaged
Under Fire
Blinded
Street Smart
Hidden Intent
Checked In

Colony Six Series
Insight (prequel)
Sketches
Visions
Travels

THIS FEELING FOR YOU

A Town Called
Forgotten

INTERNATIONAL BESTSELLING AUTHOR

RACHEL
BRANTON

WHITE
STAR
PRESS

This is a work of fiction, and the views expressed herein are the sole responsibility of the author. Likewise, certain characters, places, and incidents are the product of the author's imagination, and any resemblance to actual persons, living or dead, or actual events or locales, is entirely coincidental.

This Feeling for You (A Town Called Forgotten, Book 2)

Published by White Star Press
P.O. Box 353
American Fork, Utah 84003

Printed in the United States of America
ISBN: 978-1-948982-24-5
Year of first printing: 2020

To those who feel paralyzed with regret.
May love help you step forward out of the past.

THE SONG

This feeling for you took me by surprise,
Makes me question who I am and who I want to be.
Your laugh, your smile, your touch have changed me.
That look in your eyes tells me you feel the same.

This feeling for you.
This feeling for you . . .

This feeling for you, helpless to ignore.
Can I hold onto myself while reaching out for you?
I look for your smile, ache for your touch.
No beginning no end; there's just you and me.

This feeling for you.
This feeling for you . . .

This feeling for you is all that I know.
Sorrow and regret and pain, you slip away from me.
And I only want to be with you.
This feeling is us—real and true and endless.

This feeling for you.
This feeling for you . . .

CHAPTER 1

Maggie Tremblay knew she shouldn't have performed the song. Tasting the words and breathing the memories always brought the intoxicating mixture of joy and pain that carried her back through eighteen years to that magical day.

Usually, she indulged only on the rare solitary hike in the isolated hills of Forgotten, or in her shower after a bad day, with the television turned all the way up in the next room—as long as there were no overnight guests at her bed and breakfast café. Only then would she let herself remember and wonder why she hadn't recognized the importance of that day in Trenton or glimpsed the regrets that would haunt her for a lifetime.

Maggie had been caught singing the song in the kitchen of her café the evening before Hannah Waterford's August wedding, and one thing had led to another, and somehow she'd ended up agreeing to sing for the wedding celebration. Maybe it was because the wedding was on the thirteenth, the luckiest number in Forgotten, or maybe because the wedding dinner Maggie was responsible for was turning out perfectly, or maybe because Hannah had become more a friend than an employee, and she was so obviously in love.

Whatever the reason, Maggie had agreed. Because at that moment she'd wanted to remember, to go back to the day that had forever changed her life. The day that had launched her successful—albeit very short—singing career, and eventually led to the choice that had taken away the man she would always love.

On that day so long ago, she hadn't known the regrets she'd agonize over. Youth was her excuse—and her disbelief in love at first sight. Afterward, she'd gone on with her life, as people had to do. She no longer wasted time on what-ifs—or mostly she didn't. Those thoughts only broke through her barriers when she gave into the song.

On those days when loneliness crept into the fabric of her chosen life, she pushed the emotion aside. She couldn't have possibly felt so strongly about someone after so little time together. It wasn't conceivable. She had to be remembering the day in error.

Right?

Whatever the past and her regrets, Maggie was happy now. She loved Forgotten, Kansas, population three thousand, seven hundred eighty-six. She loved the way everyone knew her current life and cared about how she was doing. She was amazed at how people pitched in when anyone in town needed help. She liked the handsome cowboys who asked her out to county fairs and rodeos and treated her like a queen. She appreciated the country attorneys who liked to drive her to nearby Panna Creek for a nice dinner without expecting anything but a smile and good conversation in return. She loved talking with her customers, and she even enjoyed the Ladies Auxiliary, who gossiped as much as they helped anyone.

No one questioned her life before she came to Forgotten thirteen years ago. The past outside the town was not important. Only what she did now, who she was now. She was Maggie, owner of the Butter Cake Café that also doubled as a bed and breakfast with three rooms to rent, only one of which had a private bathroom. She was an employer, friend, and town leader. She made the best gooey butter cake in the entire county, and people came from neighboring cities for her steaks and soups. It was a good life. She didn't want anything to shatter her peace, especially something related to the song that she'd agreed to sing in front of everyone in a weak moment.

"Maggie, what's wrong?" Hannah asked, touching her shoulder and bringing her thoughts back to the present.

Maggie looked up from her tablet on the café counter, where she had been staring at the shares on Hannah's Twitter feed, fighting the clenching of her gut. Both her full-time employees, Hannah Morgan and Keisha Jefferson, were looking at her, their expressions concerned, and she needed to say something in response.

She waved a hand that felt stiff, as if it didn't belong to her. "Nothing. I just didn't know so many people would see me singing. It's been two and a half weeks since the wedding, and people are still sharing it and commenting. It's a little embarrassing."

No one had asked Maggie if they could record her at the wedding, but she should have known someone would do so. All the generations were caught up in technology these days. Why, oh why had she given in to the idea?

She knew the answer, of course: she'd been convinced by love. Hannah and Dylan getting married after everything they'd been through was inspiring and romantic . . . and utterly, disgustingly, annoyingly sweet. How could you not join in?

"It's only five thousand shares." Hannah smiled as she tucked a wisp of hair behind her ear that had escaped her blond ponytail, her voice dismissive, as if that number were nothing.

To Maggie, it sounded like a lot. But to be honest, Maggie didn't really know. Back in the day, social media hadn't been a thing. She should have known that as the ex-wife of a Nebraska senator, Hannah's post about her wedding so soon after the dissolution of her unhappy marriage would have attracted notice in the media. Hopefully, it would die down soon. Maybe it wouldn't even reach many people outside the US—if Maggie was lucky.

Keisha snorted and her hazel eyes sparkled. "And a million views on YouTube." She leaned over the tablet, opened the website, and typed in a few words to find the video. "They're comparing both your singing and guitar playing to the original artist, GiGi Blay. Believe me, that's a real compliment! I listened to her recording last night, and it's true. You sound just like her, or maybe even better. She's so young—at least she was back when she recorded it. She's a Canadian singer, by the way. Not much is known about her." She drew back to let Maggie see the million views on Hannah's post.

Maggie stifled a groan, which made Hannah laugh. "Don't be a grump," she said. "It's about time everyone in Forgotten knows how well you sing. I've been saying for months that you have the best voice. You should be recording songs, not slaving away here at the café."

"What do you mean? I *love* my café." And Maggie did. So

much. She had no desire to return to that other life. Unless . . . unless she could physically go back twenty years, and that wasn't happening any time soon. Time machines did not exist.

"I'm just hoping the real artist doesn't sue, or something." Keisha pulled a yellow apron over her white blouse, the combination of colors bright against her bronze skin and dark brown hair, now drawn up in a ponytail. She hadn't used hair relaxer in a few months, as she often did, and the new growth close to her scalp was full and curly, and a little bushy, just the way Maggie liked it. "Hannah might be forced to take it down."

"We'll face that if it happens." Hannah started for the kitchen. "I'll get the afternoon bread started so it can rise during the lunch rush." She was the only one who could make the bread besides Maggie. They'd perfected it together, and the Butter Cake Café sandwiches had improved over the past few months since her employ. Maggie was going to hate losing her when a teaching job finally opened up in Forgotten or nearby Panna Creek. The week Hannah had taken off for her honeymoon had been challenging enough.

Maggie nodded. "Thanks." She kept her voice light, but inside she felt sick. *A million views.*

But why did it matter? It wasn't as if *he* would see. Even if he did, he wasn't in a position to care.

Keisha studied her with serious hazel eyes. "Don't worry. In a few more days, no one will remember. It'll probably disappear, and I bet Hannah will take it down if you ask."

Right. And that was exactly what Maggie would do. She forced a smile and powered off the tablet. "Looks like your first pre-lunch customer is here. No talking about this, okay?"

Keisha nodded and put on her flirty face. She got more tips than anyone at the Butter Cake Café, though lately Maggie had been feeling some distraction in Keisha's service. She'd have to ask about that soon.

One customer turned into three, and before Maggie knew it, she was in the middle of the lunchtime crowd. The three of them could handle it easily, even with the influx of construction workers who were building the new Noodleroni factory west of Main, beyond the grade school. Once it and the accompanying housing development was completed, the population in Forgotten would go up by a few hundred. Most people were excited about the addition, including Maggie. She'd had full occupancy in her rental rooms up until a week ago, which had really helped her bottom line.

When the lunch rush ended, she drew off her apron and headed out of the kitchen. Hannah was taking a break at a table where her new husband, town vet Dylan Morgan, was still eating lunch. Keisha was at another table talking to her uncle, Mayor Josiah Campbell, who was on a bar stool finishing his own meal.

"Lunch was wonderful as always," Josiah said to Maggie in his warm voice. Setting down his napkin, he stood, towering over them. He took Maggie's hand in his very large ones, his ebony skin as dark as hers was pale. "I've been meaning to tell you that your song was beautiful. You've been hiding this talent from us, but we know you now." He winked. "In fact, Olivia is already plotting how she can get you to perform at her next evening soiree for her out-of-town friends."

"Is she now?" Maggie would find a way to be busy that night. If there was one thing in Forgotten she didn't like, it was Olivia Campbell. But like everyone else in town, Maggie put up with her because she loved and admired Josiah and Keisha.

Josiah's bright smile widened knowingly. "Don't worry. I'll give you a heads up the minute I hear of the date. I'm assuming you'll have other plans that day."

His chuckle was infectious, and Maggie laughed. "I'd appreciate that."

Josiah gave his niece a pat on the shoulder. "You come and see me when you get a minute, okay? You know where my office is. We're family, and that will never change."

"Okay." Keisha held her smile until he left the café. "Wish he were related to me by blood," she muttered, "instead of through that snotty wife of his. Seriously, the only thing she's ever done right is to marry Josiah. To his detriment, I might add. Well, and she had Charlie. I thank God every day that he's turning out like his dad. I don't know why Josiah stays with her."

Maggie had already heard hints that a breakup was on the horizon, but she wouldn't share that information with Keisha or anyone, even if she echoed the sentiments. Josiah wasn't one to give up easily, though, and he'd already fought more for his marriage than anyone she knew. Maybe he'd work things out.

"I'm going upstairs for a little nap," she said to Keisha. "Text me if it picks up too much."

"Oh, I'm sure it'll be dead until dinner," Keisha said. "It's Tuesday. But okay."

Maggie went around the counter, passing the small copy room she'd installed for guests, and made her way up the stairs leading to the next floor. She felt tired, which was normal after the unsettled night she'd had worrying about the song post. And restless night or no, she still had to be up by five-thirty every single morning except Sundays when the café was closed. Some Sundays she could sleep in as late as eight or nine if she didn't have boarders.

She had only one guest now—Connor Davis, a savvy developer

who was over both the new pasta factory and the housing development. Apparently, the trailers where the imported workers slept on-site weren't quite up to his standard for his weekly visits to Forgotten. He arrived every Sunday night and left every Tuesday or Wednesday morning, depending on his purpose. He'd also temporarily installed various managers or investors in her rooms over the past three months, which gave her a boost of funds. Since he was using a lot of local boys for the job site, helping all of Forgotten, she was inclined to be nice to him.

He was also good on the eyes, and they had passed more than one private breakfast in each other's company downstairs in her dining room. He was well-read and polite, and his flirtatious manner was flattering. Once or twice lately, she'd begun to wonder if maybe something more might come of their relationship. But he was at least five years younger, and not the kind of man to be satisfied with small-town life. Her life here was set, and she wouldn't move or give up her independence, but there were other options she'd consider—these days many couples commuted for relationships.

Her personal suite was at the end of the hall, comprised of a large sitting room, a kitchenette with a microwave and mini fridge, a bedroom with a large walk-in closet, a connected bathroom, and extra storage. In the beginning when she'd first come to Forgotten, the space in the remodeled frontier-style house had seemed incredibly large after the tiny apartment where she'd grown up and the flea-bitten motels she'd stayed in over the years while trying to break into the music business. It was even nicer than the better hotel rooms she'd been able to afford at the end. She'd used all the rest of her savings to remodel and launch the Butter Cake Café, and it was the one thing in her life she didn't regret.

Well, there was a second thing she'd never take back, but she wasn't going to think about that other one right now.

She opened the door with a key from the pocket of her jeans and hurried inside, immediately kicking off her sandals and sinking onto her vibrant mauve couch, which might not be the height of fashion but was so comfortable she didn't care. It wasn't as if she invited anyone here these days. This was her private place where she could relax the confident face she presented to the world. It wasn't a false face by any stretch, but it wasn't exactly the whole truth either.

She pulled the three separate elastics from her black hair and scrubbed her hands over her scalp, separating the ebony strands. The heavy length of her hair sometimes caused headaches, but she'd solved that by pulling up a third of her hair high on her head, adding that to a third in the middle, and finishing it all into a final elastic at the nape of her neck. That spread out the weight. The hair on her neck was a little hot for summer but tolerable for the first week of September, which was already showing signs of cooling off.

She stopped when she realized she was humming the song under her breath. *This feeling for you took me by surprise. Makes me question who I am and who I want to be . . .* Her lips pursed over the sound, shutting it away, and she stretched out on her couch and closed her eyes. Just a little nap would calm the jittery feeling inside her.

She wished she could talk to Charlotte, Forgotten's midwife and her best friend. Charlotte was the only one who knew anything about her past, and maybe she'd be able to shed a little commonsense perspective. Out of all the people and songs in the world, her tiny performance shouldn't bother her this much, so why couldn't she let it go?

The memory of those million views drove her not to call Charlotte, but to the laptop she kept on the coffee table. Sitting up, she pulled it onto her lap and stretched her legs out on the couch cushions. She'd check her email to make sure nothing had come of the exposure. Not the Butter Cake Café email she used now, but the old personal email she made sure to clean out every six months. There had only been twenty emails the last time—all spam. Even most of the spammers had given up on the address now, which said a lot. Maybe it was time to finally let the email account go. She hadn't received a fan email in at least seven years.

This time there were only nine spam emails—but there was a tenth one that set her heart thudding. She opened it with a mixture of dread, which she understood, and excitement, which she did not.

Hey G. Where are you, girl? Saw you singing on YouTube. You thinking about making a comeback? I can help. I still got the contacts in the music industry, and you still got it, babe. Always did. Let me know. No hard feelings here. Axel

So the clip had caught the attention of Ontario viewers, if that was still where Axel Zyon lived. She wondered if it had been suggested to him by the video platform or if someone had recognized her—or at least the song—and informed him because of copyright issues. Only he knew that she still owned all of her songs and that she hadn't continued licensing anyone to use them, despite his urging over the years. It hurt too much.

"Not at my age," she muttered to him.

His name brought up no additional emotions inside her, which had always been part of the problem. Axel had been her agent and friend, but he hadn't been the man she loved, and she couldn't pretend otherwise. So she'd done the only thing she could at the end—she'd hurt him, both emotionally and financially, by leaving. Could he really have forgiven her? She hoped so, but it didn't mean she'd go running back to Canada. No, Kansas was her home, or at least Forgotten was. Fewer people might know her name now, but they knew the real her.

Should she write back? For several minutes, she considered deleting the email as she had the other nine spam emails. That would be normal in his world, but this was Forgotten, and she was now a small-town girl with small-town manners.

Hey, Axel, she typed. *I'm definitely not planning a comeback. I've got a great business, and life is good. But I want you to know I appreciate all you tried to do for me. I was a mess back then, and I'm sorry. I hope you are doing well. You deserve it.*

She thought for a moment before signing it with her real name, *Maggie,* instead of her stage name, GiGi, or the pet name of G that he'd called her. Maybe this soft response would go a short way toward making up for the terse emails she'd sent to him the first few years after she'd left, if she'd answered at all.

She shut the laptop and lay back on her couch, settling into the soft folds, closing her eyes. She still wanted to talk to Charlotte, but that could wait. And maybe if an email from Axel was the only fallout from the video posting, she wouldn't ask Hannah to take it down. Her friend was so happy with her new husband, and Maggie didn't want to cast a shadow over that.

She had dozed off, her hand resting on the gold pocket watch she always wore on a chain around her neck, when her phone began to buzz on the coffee table where she'd left it. Reaching clumsily for it, she spied Keisha's phone number.

"Yeah?" she asked, her voice clogged with sleep. How long had she been out?

"Um, there's a man asking for you. Can you come down? He's someone I've never seen before."

"Did he say what it's about?"

"No. Should I tell him to leave you a note?"

Maggie sighed and swung her feet to the ground, tucking the pocket watch inside her blouse where it nestled in the valley made by her breasts. Out of sight, but always close to her heart. "No. I'll come. It's probably the new county health inspector. I'll have to deal with it, or they'll pester me. Offer him a piece of butter cake. I'll be right down."

"Good idea. Nothing like your gooey butter cake to butter someone up." Keisha's voice lowered. "Especially when he's tall, dark, and gorgeous."

Maggie laughed. "Maybe he'll leave you a good tip or ask you out."

"Not my type." The comment made Maggie wonder what Keisha's type was. Until recently, she'd energetically dated men from all over the county, but of late, she'd stopped accepting any offers. Was that when her unsettled behavior had begun? *Something's bothering her,* Maggie thought. *Something more than her aunt's annoying behavior.* Should she ask about it or wait until Keisha came to her? Maggie would have to give it some thought.

She slipped on her sandals and hurried to the door, locking it behind her. It wasn't until she reached the stairs that she remembered her hair. Well, it shouldn't matter that it wasn't tied back. She wasn't currently working, and the inspector would have to understand that.

As she reached the dining room, nodding at a solitary group of people eating at one of the tables, she saw the man on one of the barstools. He had very short, dark brown hair like a businessman, and his crisp gray shirt, black slacks, and shiny black shoes added to the impression. The set of his wide shoulders, however, was different—squared and straight like a military man.

He turned at that moment, and her breath simply stopped. It was *him*.

The room began to fade around her, and she reached out to steady herself on the edge of the counter. Only he remained solid, like an anchor in her confusion. She breathed in deeply. Was her mind playing tricks? He couldn't be here. It had to be a mistake.

He popped up from his chair as if ready to salute. It was the same face: square jaw, cleanshaven cheeks, well-molded lips, and dark blue eyes that had captured her from the first. He was older now, but his dark hair held no traces of gray.

No, she thought with a touch of desperation. *It can't be him.* She couldn't—wouldn't believe. He was an American, but the chances of Garth Dalton being in Forgotten were astronomical. It was one of the reasons she'd chosen the small town.

To hide? No, to find a way to live, to go on. And she had.

The room stopped spinning. "May I help you?" she asked.

"Maggie, don't you recognize me?" His wide smile cut through the shield around her heart like a sharp knife through her best gooey butter cake. It *was* him.

"I'd know *you* anywhere," he continued. "You look exactly the same as the day we first met." His chuckle reached all the way down inside her, stirring . . . something. "Well, different blouse. That day it was yellow, wasn't it? Your favorite color."

She didn't look the same, of course. Eighteen years had a way of taking its toll. But at that moment, she still felt like the young Canadian girl who had fallen for the American Air Force pilot stationed briefly in Trenton while preparing for his new assignment in Afghanistan, a joint US venture with Canada. Now he was here, in her town, her café. Her heart had no protection for this.

"Garth Dalton," she said, her voice surprisingly steady. "But . . . what are you doing here?"

"I saw you singing on the Internet. One of the guys texted me about it. Blew me away, seeing you like that. Brought it all back. I had some time, so I made a few calls, grabbed a flight, and here I am. What, don't I get a hug?" He took a tentative step toward her, his arms open.

As if a hug would help her floundering heart. Why didn't the ground just open up and swallow her? It would be easier. Far easier. Did he know the song was inspired by words he'd said to her on that magical day? Did he remember?

She had no choice but to step forward into his embrace, to pretend they were casual friends. She'd try to keep it to a half hug, exactly like the second and last time they'd met, surrounded by soldiers and his family. What on earth was he doing here? Why had he come at all?

Despite her effort, his arms closed around her in a real hug—tight, enthusiastic, and breath-stealing. He smelled the same as she remembered, and his touch felt exactly the way it once had. His closeness threatened to break down her remaining barriers. This was what she wanted—his arms around her, their bodies sparking fire. Was she still up on her couch dreaming? That had to be it. Yet he felt so solid, so . . . like Garth.

His lips touched her cheek, igniting a need so deep inside she didn't know if she would ever be able to excise it again. She wanted to grab him tighter and tell him all the things she should have eighteen years ago.

But she couldn't. There had been too much time, and the last she knew, he wasn't a free man. Clamping down on her emotions, she drew away.

"It's nice to see you," she said coolly—or rather, tried to say coolly. It came out a little too bright and happy, as if she'd been waiting for this day for eighteen years.

Maybe she had.

CHAPTER 2

Garth Dalton remembered exactly how Maggie Tremblay had looked the first day he'd met her on the riverfront in Trenton. Her long, glossy black hair, fanned out around her slender shoulders, had shone almost blue in the bright sunlight, and her smile had drawn him helplessly toward her.

He and the other American pilots were on leave from their temporary station at the Canadian Forces Base in Trenton before their upcoming joint assignment in Afghanistan. It was summer and Trenton was in the thick of a riverfront band festival that brought both base personnel and local residents together in a flood of music, dancing, food booths, and games. Garth's plan had been to drink a little, eat a lot, and laugh as he celebrated his last day on Canadian soil. After Afghanistan, he'd be going back home to serve in the US. Unless the war worsened, of course, or another began. No one really knew what the Taliban were capable of.

Then he'd seen Maggie, standing on a makeshift stage with a microphone in her hand, and everything in his life changed. Of course, it hadn't worked out the way he'd hoped, and holding her in his arms now brought back some of the hurt he'd experienced at her rejection then. But he couldn't allow the past to cloud his thinking. He'd come here with a reason, and he wasn't backing down: he wanted the truth of what had happened between them.

He also wanted to hold her exactly like this forever, but if that wasn't possible, he'd at least finally know why she'd walked away.

She pulled from his grasp, and he let her go. "So, Forgotten," he said. "It's a beautiful little town."

She nodded but didn't smile, as if the comment had offended her somehow. "It is. I love it here."

"That's good." He found it hard to believe, this woman who had without a thought jumped up on that riverfront stage and belted out a popular song that had thrilled thousands in the crowd— and had attracted the attention of a talent scout. She'd been only eighteen then, barely out of school. So many years ago.

She was more beautiful now. Her figure was fuller in the right places, marking the difference between girl and woman. Her eyes were deep and dark and kind, and her voice the same silky, slightly husky, sexy lilt that had driven him wild. Somehow, she was both earthy and ethereal. Touchable, but oh-so-hard to reach. A moment of panic swept through him. What was he doing here? Why did he think this meeting would come out any differently?

His Air Force training came to his aid. If he could fly a plane into enemy territory and rescue soldiers and civilians, he could face Maggie. If he could defy a direct order to save half a dozen children, he could find out why she'd turned from him all those years ago.

Maggie's dark eyes went past him to the young woman beyond the counter, who seemed to be waiting on them. "This is Garth Dalton, an old friend." Her voice faltered only slightly on the word friend, but that falter gave him hope. Once, they'd been so much more than friends. But he needed to tread carefully now, and even though she was using her maiden name, there might be a husband in the wings. If that was the case, he'd have to move on. Again.

"Nice to meet you," the woman said, her smile wide and bright against her brown skin. "I'm Keisha. You saw the YouTube video?"

He nodded, barely able to drag his eyes from Maggie. "Yeah. Whoever put it together did a good job."

"That would be Hannah." Keisha thumbed to the open doorway leading into what he assumed was the kitchen, where they could hear but not see someone clinking pans. "Apparently, it's a hobby she picked up as an elementary teacher. Guess videos attract kids' attention."

"Just my luck," Maggie muttered. The sides of her mouth quirked up in a way Garth remembered only too well. But there was no real mirth in her face. She obviously hadn't wanted the video posted, so maybe she preferred to keep the past in the past. Maybe she didn't look back with regret like he did every single day. Even when he was in his happy place, flying in the sky, up high where he almost felt he could touch God, the regret was there like a tiny, solid lump of blackness in his soul.

"It was lucky," Garth said firmly. "Especially now, when I have time to visit."

"You're on leave?" Maggie asked.

"Actually, I just retired from the Air Force. I'll still probably end up flying somewhere, but not for the government."

"No way." The doubt in Keisha's eyes was apparent. "You don't look old enough for that."

He grinned. "I put in twenty years. I was young when I started. Wasn't I, Maggie?" His gaze went back to her as if pulled by some unseen force. She was so beautiful.

"Yes, you were," she agreed. "You hungry?"

"Naw. I stopped in Panna Creek on my way here. I didn't know . . ." He didn't know what kind of reception he'd get, and he still had no idea. "If you're not too busy," he added. "I'd love to see your town."

Maggie didn't respond for several seconds, during which his heartbeat tripled. What if she said no? What if he'd come all this way, and his efforts were a bust?

Maggie looked down at her clothes. "Sure, but I'm working later."

"Take your time." Keisha covered a yawn as she pulled a stool to the end of the counter and sat in front of the cash register. "Like I predicted, we're dead. Hannah and I can handle anything we'll get, at least until dinner."

"Well, call me if that changes." Maggie looked pointedly at Garth before taking a step toward the front door of the café.

Garth hesitated, looking at the half-eaten piece of butter cake on his plate. It was delicious, but another bite might make him queasier than he already was at wondering if Maggie wished he'd never come.

Misinterpreting his hesitation, Keisha grabbed a napkin and scooped the cake onto it with a fork. "There," she said, handing it to him. "Have fun, you two."

Cake in hand, Garth followed Maggie out the front door to the cobbled walkway that ran the entire length on both sides of Forgotten Main Street. He knew he should find it quaint and beautiful, but all he could think of was that this town had taken her from him.

No, that had happened long before, when he was in Afghanistan. She hadn't given him her number the day they'd met, no matter how many times he'd asked over the twenty-six hours they'd spent together, and it had taken him a year to track her down through his Canadian buddies at the Trenton base. The many emails he and Maggie exchanged then had him hopeful, but she'd cut it off after only two months, right after her hit single "This Feeling for You" reached the top of the charts.

So he'd gone on with his life. What other choice had there been? And if he'd flown a bit more dangerously, or risked more during operations, it had only brought him more attention and promotions. After another two years, he was sent back to the states, and there he'd met Ivy. At twenty-five, marriage hadn't really been on his mind, but she had a two-year-old daughter, and it seemed the honorable thing to do. They'd been happy enough, and life had been good. For a time.

"So," Maggie said into the heavy silence that hung between them, "how much time do you have? I'm assuming you have another flight?"

Garth's insides shivered at the silkiness of her voice. But she was so serious now, not like the laughing girl she'd been. "I don't have a return flight yet," he said, "or any place I need to be. I only retired two months ago. I'm still enjoying the freedom."

She laughed at that, and a contented warmth slid over him. "I doubt you'll be able to keep away from a plane for long," she said.

"No," he said with a chuckle. "Probably not." But he was no longer the young pilot who had craved dangerous adventure. The yearning for the open skies was there—he assumed it always would be—but it was different now. He wanted more. "I've been thinking about doing private charters with a company. Or maybe work for the airlines, but I'm tired of schedules for the moment, and with my retirement pay and savings, there's really no hurry."

She arched a brow. "I thought you liked schedules and all that. You always had a lot to say about the pilots who didn't follow the rules."

She was right, but that was before he'd learned for himself that sometimes you had to step outside the box to save lives and protect freedoms. "Guess I grew up."

They were passing a park next to the café, and he purposefully took a step closer to her. Her eyes caught on his face, not missing the motion. She'd always been able to read him right from the start, and it was another reason he'd fallen so hard for her. But she'd laughed that first day when he'd told her he loved her, saying she didn't believe in love at first sight and how she wasn't going to put her life on hold for a soldier.

He'd felt that twenty-six hours of talking and laughing and loving hadn't been first sight—it had been crazy and wonderful and unlike anything he'd ever experienced. If he hadn't been scheduled to fly out the next day, he would have stayed with her and tried harder to make her understand.

Maggie turned down a cobbled path into the park itself, stepping away from him and increasing the distance between them. "How's your family?"

He knew without her saying so that she was asking about Ivy. "My parents are good," he said. "They're still living in Florida, and so is my brother. He's in real estate now. He and his wife have three kids—all boys. I bought a condo there last month."

She waited for more, but he had nothing more he wanted

to share. He felt embarrassed that despite his efforts, Ivy had left him when her daughter, Cora, was eleven. By then, he was staying with her more for Cora's sake than anything. That she'd left him for Cora's birth father, who spent only two days every month with Cora, was something he'd never fully understood.

"Ivy and I went our separate ways six years ago," he said finally, because of course Maggie needed to know if there could be any chance between them.

She stopped and studied him. "I'm sorry."

"Well, it was for the best. I miss Cora, though."

"You don't see your daughter?" There was a hint of censure in her voice that he couldn't miss.

"Sometimes. I don't have custody, though, and Ivy moved to St. Louis after the divorce." He still remembered when the judge ruled that it wouldn't be in Cora's best interest to continue seeing Garth since she already had two biological parents who would be in her life. Never mind that Garth had raised her since she was two and considered himself her "real" father. Instead, he'd been forced to take on the role of uncle who sent presents for birthdays or who took her to an amusement park whenever he was in town.

"You didn't have more children?"

A stab of pain ran through him. "No," he said shortly.

She regarded him without comment for a few seconds before turning to walk again, saying nothing when he needed her to say nothing. She'd been that way too when they'd met, particularly when she'd asked about his father, leaving it until he was ready to talk. And it hadn't taken long for him to tell her about his Dad's upset at his willingness to risk his life by joining the Air Force, especially when he was already halfway through his aviation degree to become a commercial pilot. Maggie's own airman father had abandoned her family while she was still a young child, and her advice about being grateful that his father cared enough to fight for him was something Garth had never forgotten. He and his father had patched things up eventually, and his dad was his proudest supporter now.

"I never told you thanks for telling me to be patient with my dad," he said into the silence that had grown awkward between them.

"He came around?"

"Took a few years, but yes. He's still relieved I'm retired, though."

She laughed. "I am too."

Did that mean she still cared? Could she feel the same push toward him that he'd felt the instant he'd seen her new video on YouTube? "I thought my being a pilot was attractive back in the day."

"*Back* being the operative word," she said. "Daring excitement is for the youth, I think."

Garth wasn't so sure. Coming here felt a lot more dangerous than his mission in Afghanistan and even the ones he'd later flown in Iraq. "You look pretty young to me," he said.

Without responding, she led him up the steps of a large, white gazebo situated in the middle of the park. White-painted bench seats lined the edges, and she chose one to sit on. "This is my favorite place on Main Street," she said. "At some point in the day, a lot of people end up here when they come to buy groceries at Terrell's, and on Sundays after church people come here to talk." She motioned across the street, where he could see the grocery store opposite the park and the church on its right, across from Maggie's café.

He settled on the bench with a foot of space between them. "It's peaceful." Tall trees shaded the walkways that wound across the large stretch of newly cut grass. There were even a few stone tables for people to play chess, one of which was occupied at the moment by a tall, muscular, dark-skinned man and a frail, pale, white-haired senior.

"That's our mayor, Josiah Campbell," Maggie said, seeing his gaze. "He's Keisha's uncle. The older man is Fletcher Wilson." Her face flushed slightly. "Not that you needed to know that."

But he wanted to know everything about her and the town that had captured her. "It looks like fun. I learned to play chess in Iraq during our downtime."

"I know how to play, but I'm no good. Little too sedentary for me."

He smiled at that before unwrapping the napkin from his piece of cake and biting into it again. It tasted great now that his worry had abated. He swallowed his mouthful and said, "So, you own a café now."

Her dark eyes narrowed. "You've done your research."

"Maybe." He'd made a dozen calls before he'd come. "But the fact that you have a room at the café and the way your employee talked about you, I would have known it was yours anyway." He paused, taking another bite and letting a little silence come between them before adding, "I was surprised you stopped singing. You were sure a hit at the base that day." It had been the last time he'd seen her.

That had been, what? Almost fourteen years ago? His superiors had wanted to raise morale at the Texas base where he was stationed, and he'd suggested inviting GiGi Blay to perform. Why not? She was popular, he happened to have her email address, and he knew for himself that she could hold a crowd. When she'd accepted the invitation and came to the base, he'd been both pleased and shaken. Pleased because she remembered him and shaken because the moment he'd seen her, he'd known he wasn't over her, that he was still playing through the what-ifs in his mind—even with Ivy at his side. By then Maggie was engaged to her agent, who seemed a perfect match for her. If that wasn't closure, he didn't know what was.

Seeing Maggie again hadn't started the decline of his marriage; rather, it had almost saved it. He'd already realized that his marriage, barely more than a year old, wasn't all he'd hoped, and he had rededicated himself to the relationship. For seven more years he'd tried—oh, how he'd tried. Until he'd finally understood that Ivy had other plans. That last year in Texas together had been torturous for both of them. In the end, he'd given her the house in the divorce, and her quick remarriage and the custody judgment had saved him years of alimony. He should have counted himself lucky, but she'd sold the house and moved Cora to St Louis, as if hoping to permanently cut off all ties. The years that followed had him volunteering for missions and pushing for active assignments to keep the regrets at bay. For a time, he'd even gone back to living on base. He'd learned to look forward instead of backward and to make the best of what his choices had brought him.

All of that shattered when he'd received the email from his buddy, and Maggie's face had appeared on his computer screen, coming at a time when he was at a crossroads with his future. The old yearning had resurfaced, which he knew meant his closure wasn't so closed after all.

"Being in the limelight isn't all people think," Maggie said, dragging his mind back to the here and now. "People never see the flea-bitten hotels, the backstabbing, the side of the life that can drag you down."

"You never married?"

"Almost. But I realized it wouldn't work."

Why? he wanted to ask. Instead, he said, "Lucky you."

"Well, you have Cora."

"Yeah. There is that." Cora was now an angry, seven-teen-year-old, who somehow blamed him for any problems she had with her parents, which, up until a few months ago, she used to call to tell him about in detail.

He stretched to throw away the napkin in a small white garbage container next to the bench, his gaze catching on the men playing chess. They both had a story, a life, just like he did, and for a minute he was compelled to know it. Were they happy? Was anyone ever happy with the choices they'd made, or did they always long for something out of reach?

He turned to see Maggie watching him. "Why are you really here?" she asked softly.

Her words wrapped around his heart like a vise-grip. Should he tell her? Should he say that he still dreamt of their day together and that his heart had never healed? That he longed to hold her in his arms—or to rid himself of the desire once and for all? She was either an angel who might save him or a temptress who would break his heart.

Again.

Except she had not sought him out, so his being here wasn't her fault. He should walk away now and never look back.

"I'm here because I wanted to see you." His voice came out husky but sure. He slid closer to her on the wooden bench. "Because I've always wondered what might have happened if I hadn't left Trenton."

Her eyes became twin brown storms in the calm of her face. "You had no choice."

"I know." And he'd wanted to go to Afghanistan, to finally

fight and do something for his country. The boy he'd been hadn't understood what he'd have to give up, the pieces of his soul he'd leave behind in that foreign country. That had nothing to do with Maggie but everything to do with why he was here. He had learned to recognize what was important in life, and craving the way she'd made him feel was right up there with food and shelter. Their relationship was something he could attempt to right.

"Garth," she said, her head shaking slowly. "You shouldn't have come."

"You want me to leave?" It hurt to say the words, but he would leave if she asked. Not because of pride but for honor. Honor was another thing he'd learned a lot about in the past eighteen years. He hadn't always been honorable with her, and it was one of his biggest regrets.

When she didn't tell him to leave, a sliver of hope shot into his soul.

"I don't even know you," she said with a faint smile. "And you don't know me. It was one day."

"And the emails." More than a thousand emails to be exact. He'd shared his whole life with her. He took her hand and placed it over his heart. "And, yes, you do know me." She might be the only one who did—or who once had.

For an eternal moment they stared at each other, his heart beating against her hand through the thin material of his shirt. He could see an answering throbbing in her long, white neck. He'd kissed that neck once, and the memory was seared into his mind.

All too soon, she pulled her hand away, leaving a blistering heat in his chest. "Eighteen years is a lifetime." Her voice was scarcely a whisper. "I'm a different person now, and so are you."

"A big part of me is still that cocky, young pilot," he said. "But in case you've forgotten him, I think I'll stick around awhile, if you don't mind. Maybe we can get to know each other again. Do you have a room I can rent?"

He could see in her eyes that she wanted to say no. Was it because she really didn't want him there or because maybe, like him, she was afraid of the obstacles they would have to face to get to the other side of whatever this would become?

"I could go to a hotel instead," he added. "If you'd rather."

A faint sigh escaped her lips. "I do have a room. But we can't change the past."

Logically, she was right, but right now his heart was one of a twenty-two-year-old pilot who had fallen in love with the most fascinating woman he'd ever met.

"Then let's start at the beginning and make a new past," he said.

Her only response was to stand and leave the gazebo, heading back to the café.

CHAPTER 3

Maggie could sense Garth following her, hurrying his steps to catch up. With his long strides, it didn't take long. Why hadn't she told him to leave? Having him here would only dig at the old sores that had taken years to close.

But didn't he deserve to know the truth?

No. Not when he hadn't been the person he'd pretended to be. Not when it looked like he'd abandoned his daughter, if not his wife. Maybe that was his true self.

And what was her true self? She had kept every bit as much from him as he had from her. Perhaps far more. She regretted it now. So much. But nothing she could do would change her past choices, and some things you couldn't make up for.

She was focusing so much on the cobblestones that she would have barreled into Ronica Wilson if Garth hadn't put a hand on her upper arm to slow her movement. His touch tantalized her even through the half sleeve of her white blouse.

"Oh," she said, letting out a breath.

"Sorry." Ronica laughed as they both stopped abruptly. "I wasn't paying attention."

"My fault," Maggie said. Ronica and her husband Fletcher had been regulars at her café every morning up until the past month when the Alzheimer's disease that was slowly absorbing Fletcher's life had become more prominent. They'd been at the café this morning, which meant it was a better day, and the fact that the mayor was playing chess with Fletcher instead of working in his office hinted that Ronica was planning the next city event, which the city employed her to do when she wasn't busy helping her son on the family farm.

"It's okay." Ronica's short brown hair was perfectly in place, and her blue eyes were happy, though dealing with her husband's dementia had taken a lot of her usual perkiness from her step. She looked younger than her fifty-two years, however, and somehow she kept abreast of almost everything that happened in town, from a new baby to broken pipes. If you needed information, Ronica was the woman to ask.

Garth and Ronica both looked at Maggie expectantly, waiting for introductions. "Oh, Garth, this is a friend, Ronica Wilson," Maggie said. "Ronica, I'd like you to meet Garth Dalton. He's staying at the Butter Cake for a few days."

"Oh." Ronica looked a little disappointed at the short explanation, and so did Garth, though he didn't refute Maggie's claim.

But why should he? This was her town, and whatever his ultimate intention, if he wanted her cooperation, it would have to be on *her* terms. She certainly would not be introducing him as an old boyfriend.

He shook Ronica's hand. "Nice to meet you."

"You too." Ronica smiled and then pried in typical Ronica fashion, "How long will you be here?"

"I'm not sure yet. I'm between jobs, you might say."

Ronica grinned. "Not much to do here in town, unless you're a farmer or rancher." Her eyes ran the length of his body, slender but obviously taut and muscled. Maggie fought down a flare of ridiculous jealousy.

"No, I'm a pilot," Garth said. "Just retired from the Air Force, actually."

"Really, that's very interesting." Ronica's eyes took on a new light, and Maggie imagined the mileage she'd get when telling the story. "My husband used to—" But whatever Ronica was going to say, she stopped. Maybe because Fletcher no longer remembered what he used to do. Fletcher had become like a sweet, absent-minded child instead of the tough, savvy farmer he'd once been.

Ronica gave her head a shake. "Never mind. But speaking of him, I'm here to pick him up. Josiah was kind enough to keep track of him while I worked on plans for the Harvest Festival."

"Right, the Harvest Festival," Maggie murmured. The town of Forgotten held it late every September, complete with singing in the streets, hay throwing contests, cornhusk art, food, a reenactment of the original settlers, and fireworks. For them it was bigger than the 4th of July. "You need any help?"

"Just be at the Ladies Auxiliary meeting next week," Ronica said. "We'll pass out the assignments there. We've got plenty of time."

"Okay."

Ronica refocused on Garth. "Well, I hope you enjoy your stay in Forgotten. I'll catch you later." With another bright smile,

Ronica continued in the direction of Josiah and Fletcher. Her step was light, and Maggie envied the woman her endurance.

While Ronica had been with them, Maggie had only wanted to get away, but now she found herself wishing the woman had lingered. Given a little time, Ronica would have pried Garth's entire life story out of him, from his Air Force service to his marriage and divorce, without Maggie having to say a word. She did want to know it all, but getting there seemed too dangerous.

"Nice lady," Garth said as they started off again.

"Yeah, really nice." There was a lot more she could say, but there was enough gossip in Forgotten without Maggie adding to it. She simply said, "She plans all the city events. Does a great job." Garth would be long gone before the festival, so it didn't really matter. Maggie was just making sounds—anything to hide the clenching of her stomach, which threatened to take over her entire body.

"We're not going to see the rest of the town?" Garth said, noting their trajectory toward the café.

"Oh, right. There's really not much to see. But let's go." She turned and headed the other direction. "Main Street's really quaint with the cobblestones and the line of small trees. At night, the streetlamps come on. It's like something out of an old movie. But that's only on Main Street. All the rest of the streets are like any other small town. Everything you might need is here or on the next two streets over either way. All within walking distance."

"I rented a car. Or a Jeep, rather."

"Well, then you might want to check out Forgotten Reservoir later on. It's one of the biggest attractions here."

"Will you come with me?"

Her heart banged in her chest. She should tell him her secret now before he took his things up to one of her rooms. Before her heart had a chance to . . . to what? She needed to stop right there. "Sure, I can show you the lake sometime."

His smile caused the clenching in her stomach to lessen. "I thought you said it was a reservoir."

"Right. It was a lake that was enlarged, so now it's a reservoir. We use the term interchangeably. But I don't think I'll be able to go today." She was planning on a movie tonight with Connor Davis, her remaining boarder, and it wasn't likely she could get away before then. After could be a possibility, but that meant she'd have to tell Garth about the date in the first place. *It's none of his business,* she thought.

Her hand went instinctively to the pocket watch inside her shirt to check the time but stopped short. She didn't want questions about the watch, and Keisha would call if she were needed. Besides, the current time wasn't the reason she didn't want to go to the lake with him today—or ever.

They were nearing Dream Cream, the ice cream parlor next to the park. Garth stared at the store, stopping in front of it. "You know what? This reminds me of—"

"Milk It Ice Cream in Trenton. I know." She laughed. "Sadly, Milk It is closed down now. They closed years ago, in fact." She'd checked the last time she'd been there, shortly before moving to Forgotten. "It's a sewing store now."

"Let's go inside."

He was so eager that she hesitated only for a few seconds. "Okay."

She ordered a waffle cone with a scoop of mint chocolate chip—still her favorite—while he ordered a scoop each of pecan, strawberry, and chocolate. "My treat," he said when she reached for her wallet.

Back on the street, they walked together, enjoying the ice cream. "All we need now is music in the streets and a crowd."

Re-creating their day together in Trenton was definitely not on her to-do list. "Trenton was way larger than Forgotten, even back then."

"There is that."

Increasing her pace, she took him past several more shops, the movie theater, the pizzeria, the police station, and City Hall, where he spent some time looking at the wood cabin on the grounds that had once belonged to the founders of Forgotten.

"So how did you end up here?" he asked as they walked out of the cabin. "Little far from Canada."

"Well, I was already in the states because of my music." A chance at US citizenship was the only thing her worthless American father had left her. That and a lot of resentment. "But the reason I ended up here in Forgotten was because of the café. I was originally going to find something in Canada closer to my mom, but I fell in love with the café online and had to come see it. Once I did, I didn't really have a choice. The outside was amazing, and I loved the history of it. The location next to the park and across from the church was perfect. I've done a lot of work on the inside, of course, and I also added the garage and extended my suite out over it."

What she didn't tell him was that the name of the town had appealed to her younger self. All she'd wanted to do at the time was to forget.

"I can see why you love it. It used to be a residential house, right? Like the houses on the other side of yours."

"That's right, though it was probably somewhat of a mansion for this town back in the day. A few other old houses also now contain businesses. They designed City Hall to look like it was here originally, but you can tell it's a lot newer. And larger, of course." She followed him to the small courtyard in front of City Hall, where a clock stood on a tall pedestal. The hourly chimes could be heard throughout the town all day until ten, when they were turned off for the night, except on special occasions.

"It's got ambiance, that's for sure." He fell silent as he read the plaque about the clock being donated fifty years ago by Forgotten's Ladies Auxiliary and the Morgan Foundation, which was made up of descendants of the original founders. "How's your mom?"

"Good. She stopped drinking. She's on husband number five, but they've been together fifteen years now, and she seems really content. That's another reason why I came here. She was planning to move to Calgary, and I didn't see the point of going back to Trenton when I'd be closer to her here." With her mother's step-grandchildren also in Calgary, she never even bugged Maggie about her choice to remain single.

"How did she feel about you leaving the music industry?"

"Relieved, I think." Maggie hadn't asked for advice at the time, a fact for which she now felt guilty. Her mother had been far from perfect, but she was still her mother, and she'd pulled herself together by then. "She really loves that I use her soup recipes. She's always sending me new ones to tweak and try." She paused a moment before rushing on, "I think I'd better get back to the café. But you can stay and investigate more if you want." She motioned to the building in front of them. "They have brochures inside." If he stayed here, maybe the walk back alone would give her time to adjust to his being in town.

"I'll go back with you. I'd like to get settled."

"Okay. Sure." On the way back to the café, Maggie felt on display as they passed the curious eyes of Forgotten's residents.

They stopped three times for more introductions, including that of Mayor Josiah Campbell, who was returning to work after his extended break with Fletcher Wilson.

Back at the café, only two tables were filled with customers. Keisha was reading a large, thick book at the counter. She'd been doing a lot of that lately, but Maggie didn't mind when everything was clean and no customers needed her attention.

Keisha beamed at them. "That didn't take long. But then our town isn't very big."

"Everyone's so friendly," Garth said.

Keisha laughed. "Oh, you'll get sick of that real fast. People are always in your business. In fact, the only reason I have any customers right now is because news is already spreading about the handsome Air Force captain." She thumbed at the two tables in the left part of the café without looking in their direction.

Sure enough, all the occupants were staring at them. Three of them were single women, Maggie noted sourly, including Ayleen Jenkins and Laina Cox, who were in the Ladies Auxiliary with her. Both happened to be around a decade younger than Maggie.

"Lieutenant Colonel, actually," Garth corrected, his face flushing.

Keisha gave a flirtatious giggle. "I have no idea what that means."

Garth grinned. "Apparently, nothing much. Not anymore. It's just a rank."

Ayleen and Laina were rising, as if preparing to come over to introduce themselves. "Do you have a suitcase?" Maggie interrupted. "I can show you to your room."

"Sure. I'll be right back." Pivoting on his heel, Garth headed toward the back door of the café, thankfully in the opposite direction of the customers.

Maggie went around the counter as Keisha slid from her stool. Maggie caught the barest edge of the deep scar on Keisha's right leg where her denim shorts rode up on her thigh before she smoothed it down. Four years ago, Keisha's car accident had cut short her last year of college. She'd been in the hospital for two months and had taken a year to recover fully. Since her parents' home in Forgotten had been destroyed by the fire that had taken their lives in Keisha's last month of high school, she'd had to stay with her father's half-sister, Olivia Campbell, the mayor's wife. Keisha and Olivia had never gotten along, but the will to resist had gone out of Keisha, and she'd submitted without protest. Everyone knew she had been planning to attend law school and become an attorney like her father, but she hadn't returned to school. She'd taken a job at the Butter Cake after a year of recovery only so she could move out of her aunt's home. Maggie had known it would be temporary, but three years later, Keisha was still here—the best employee Maggie had ever hired. Now Maggie wondered if the difference she felt in Keisha meant that maybe she was finally getting itchy feet.

About time, Maggie thought. Aloud, she asked, "Where's Hannah?"

"Oh, I forgot to tell you." Keisha grinned with excitement. "She left right after you did. Maria Ramos went into labor, so the school called Hannah to get her started on substituting until Maria is back from maternity leave. I'm surprised you didn't hear about it already from someone on your walk."

Maggie groaned inwardly. That was what she got for hiring a trained teacher, but she'd known it was coming since the school had already asked Hannah several months ago to fill in when the time came. As long as there had been no teacher openings in Forgotten or nearby Panna Creek, Hannah didn't have a better option than the café, but now with her foot in the educational door, it was only a matter of time before she left permanently.

"Good," Maggie said firmly. "I'm glad. It's what she wanted."

"Actually, I think she'd prefer elementary school, but high school social studies should be interesting at least. The girls will mimic her, and half the boys will be in love. Not a bad thing, since she's so sweet."

One of Maggie's teenage employees was asking for more hours and could take up the evening slack, but Maggie would have to hire someone to help cover the lunch rush. And with Hannah gone, all the bread-making would be back on Maggie's job list. She didn't really mind. In fact, maybe with Garth in town, staying busy would be best for both of them.

"How long is your friend going to stay?" Keisha asked as if reading her mind.

"No idea." Maggie's tone must have warded Keisha off because she only shrugged and shut her book without further probing. "Chemistry?" Maggie asked, catching sight of the book's title.

Keisha chewed on her lip. "Yeah, I didn't really want to say anything, but I've been taking online classes. Thought it might be time to finish my degree."

"That's fantastic." Maggie hugged her. "Way to go!"

"I don't usually need to study during the day, but this is an advanced course, and I don't want to get a bad grade."

"Don't worry about it. If you need time off, let me know. I'll figure something out." Maggie didn't see what chemistry had to do with law, but maybe it was an elective or it didn't matter what kind of degree you earned before going to law school.

"Thanks. I appreciate it. But would you mind keeping this quiet? Josiah knows because he had to help me get access to the education funds my parents left in my trust fund, but I don't want my aunt hounding me. I know you don't blab like most people here, but you might not realize I don't want it out."

"No problem." Maggie imitated closing her mouth with a zipper. "I kind of feel the same way about Garth." What was taking him anyway?

"You mean tall, dark, and pilot-y?" Keisha grinned, her eyes wide and innocent. "As far as I know, he's just a guy passing through town."

"Thanks. Look, I'm going upstairs to make sure his room is ready. Can you point him in the right direction when he comes?" She had an outside set of stairs going to the rooms, which would bypass the dining area, but he'd need a key.

"Sure." Keisha set down her book and grabbed a tub and a rag. "Looks like the ladies are finished. They'd better have tipped me well if they think they are going to wait around for any information." She winked at Maggie, who forced a smile and hurried away.

Maggie certainly wasn't going to stick around for questions about Garth. If he came back before Laina or Ayleen finished pumping Keisha for information, they were welcome to him.

CHAPTER 4

Garth opened up the back of his rented Jeep Wrangler. Bright red was the only color they'd had available in Topeka, and at first he had thought it ostentatious. But it was slowly growing on him. Maybe that's because flashy or at least a show of confidence was necessary for a pilot—at least in the beginning. He'd learned a lot about patience and real confidence over the years, but seeing Maggie again . . . well, it brought him back to the days when he had been unsure of his abilities and feared that a single bad mission might have him doing grunt runs for months.

Seeing Maggie had also brought back the reckless part of him that wouldn't stop until she was his. Of course that had never really happened, not in the way he wanted. That same passion had driven him onward to each new rank until finally he didn't want any more.

Now here he was, staring down at the new black rolling duffle he'd bought to replace the worn military bags he'd hauled all over the world. It didn't even feel as if the bag was his. Half of the clothes were also new, replacing the uniforms he'd worn every day.

His phone rang before he could pull out the duffle, and he reached for the phone in the back pocket of his slacks. He wouldn't talk now, especially not to tell any of his buddies or his family that he was out chasing the past, but one glance at the caller ID, and he changed his mind. He pressed the green icon.

"Hey, Cora."

"Hi, Garth. Good, you answered. I need your help."

"What's up?" he said, detecting upset in her voice. "Are you okay?"

"No. I hate living here with mom. I hate this school." The words came in a rush.

"I thought you said you loved it." He wracked his brain to cover their last in-person conversation. It had been the first of July, two months ago, when he visited her in St. Louis after his retirement. She'd seemed happy and excited about her upcoming senior year. When he'd invited her to spend a few weeks in his new Florida condo, she'd rolled her eyes and declared that she'd never leave her friends.

"I'm not in the same school." Her voice became hoarse with tears. "Mom and Dad split up, and Mom moved us to Arnold. She said it was going to be so cool here, but it's not. I've only been in school a week, and it's absolutely horrid, horrid, horrid. I hate being the new kid, especially in my senior year, and Mom doesn't care."

"What about living with your Dad?" Moving a child in their last year of school sounded pretty drastic. Didn't officials allow kids to claim either parent when it came to a choice between schools?

"The school would let me stay, but I don't have a way to get there. Mom can't drive me because she has to be at work before I even leave. Dad's closer, and he might be able to work out a way, but he doesn't have custody, and Mom won't let me live with him because of his new girlfriend."

His stomach sank. A part of him might be tempted to smirk at the wheels of justice, but not when it caused Cora pain. "I'm sorry. That really stinks. But what would you like me to do?"

"I want you to make her take me back to my school. I hate it here. Please, Dad."

Dad. She hadn't called him that since Garth and Ivy's divorce. Having her biological father back in her life on a daily basis, and not seeing Garth almost at all, had cured her of that habit. What child needed two dads?

"I'll talk to your mother." Not that it would do any good. The court had already ruled that he had no rights when it came to Cora.

"Then can I at least come stay with you? Please?"

"Um, I'm not sure how that's going to help you get back with your friends."

"It'll at least serve her right. You know, show her I'm serious. Please?"

No matter how much he considered, Ivy would never agree to such a thing. "I'll talk to your mother. But I'm not in Florida right now."

"Where are you? I thought you retired from the Air Force. You're always gone when I need you." The whining in her voice reminded him of her eighth birthday when his squadron had been called up and he'd missed her party. He'd made it up to her later, but she probably didn't remember that.

"I *am* retired. But I'm visiting an old friend in a little town called Forgotten. It's in Kansas."

"How long are you going to be there?"

"I'm not sure yet. Maybe a week. But I promise I'll talk to your mother as soon as I can." He pulled his duffle from the Jeep and slammed the rear door shut.

"Sure you will. A week is forever. I'm already a social outcast. You're just like Mom. You don't care about me!" The line went dead.

Her response stung, but he didn't blame her as much as her parents. The Cora he'd helped raise would never have been so disrespectful. They'd had rules and mutual esteem, but she'd been out of his house too long to remember that.

He sighed and called Ivy, leaning up against the shiny red surface of the Jeep, the strap of the duffle over one shoulder. She answered on the third ring. "It's not a good time," she said.

He rolled his eyes and made his voice pleasant. "Hello to you too."

"What do you want?"

"Cora called me."

"So I guess you know all about my divorce from Robert. I told her not to tell you. It's none of your business."

Garth fought down annoyance. "Well, you'll be happy to know that Cora hasn't breathed a word of it until today, though she's been perfectly happy to tell me about any other time you two have fought over the years." He took a deep breath to calm himself. "It becomes my concern when she asks to come live with me because she hates it so bad where she is now."

A pregnant pause and then, "She'll get used to it. She's just being stubborn. You know how she gets."

"Not really. You've done a pretty good job of keeping her away from me these past six years." That would include canceled visits when an exciting family trip came up or when friends suddenly invited Cora to do something. He knew Ivy was behind it.

"I'm only trying to do what's best for *my* daughter."

Garth couldn't address that without making her angry, and to be fair, Ivy had always been there for Cora one hundred percent, so he bit back a snarky response. Pushing off the Jeep, he started across the parking lot to a cobbled path that led back to the café. The structure of the building was roughly L-shaped, as if the back half of the house and one side had been extended—probably the garage and suite addition Maggie had mentioned. This design left a cozy alcove of path and grass up to the back entrance, which featured two outside tables that overlooked the park but weren't visible from either of the streets bordering this corner lot. An outside staircase went up to the second floor, and he wondered if it led directly to the rental rooms. He'd have to ask.

"Look, isn't there any way she can go back to her other school? It's her last year," he said, refocusing on his conversation.

"No." Ivy's curt response was practiced and immediate.

"Is this because of what happened with Robert? Because Cora shouldn't be caught in the middle of that."

"Partly." Reluctance dripped from the word.

He paused at one of the outside tables and sat, dropping his bag to the ground. "Then what about getting her a car? She could drive herself."

"And reward her for her horrible behavior? You wouldn't believe the names she's called me."

"She didn't do that when we were together." The words came out before he could stop them.

"She was a child then, not a teen. You have no idea how hard it is raising a teenager."

The words hurt because she was right. That choice had been taken from him.

"Besides, I can't afford a dependable car right now, and I can't have it breaking down."

"What about asking Robert?"

"No. He only gave me full custody if I don't make him pay anything extra."

No surprise there. Robert had never paid his share of the expenses, at least according to Cora. The house where they'd lived in St. Louis had been a box compared to the house Garth had bought her in Texas, and he had no idea what had become of the excess proceeds from the sale.

"I could help with a car," he said.

"I'm not asking for your help."

"I know that. I'm offering. I'm also open to having her stay with me for a while if you need a break."

Ivy snorted. "I didn't fight for custody just to give it up to you."

"I didn't say anything about custody. It's only if you need a break. No strings." Garth lowered his voice as a man in jeans and a T-shirt came striding up the walk from the parking lot. His skin was chestnut, his black hair trimmed short, and he wore one of those ultra-short goatees that Garth knew took more upkeep than he was willing to invest. The stranger looked more like the corporate type than a small-town cowboy, as if he'd be more comfortable in a suit than the jeans he wore.

The man nodded at Garth and gave him a smile, which Garth returned. People sure were friendly here. He liked that.

Instead of going into the back door of the café, the man headed up the outside stairs. Maybe he was staying at the café too. Or maybe—his gut clenched—or maybe he was Maggie's boyfriend.

"Look, you don't understand," Ivy said. "It's not just the divorce. At her other school, Cora was hanging out with a crowd that . . . well, they're trouble-making anarchists. I didn't like the changes I was starting to see in her. The school here in Arnold is calmer, more conservative. I feel it's what she needs right now."

So that was the real issue, one Garth couldn't refute. His connection with the military made him fiercely proud of America, and the last thing he'd want for Cora was to have her mixed up in propaganda that would destroy her future.

"Look, I appreciate you letting me know that she called, but I've got this." Despite the words, Ivy sounded anything but grateful.

"I know you're frustrated," he said, keeping his voice mild. "But maybe don't get upset with Cora for calling me. It's good for her to rage at someone besides you for a change, and I'm on your side. I've always been on your side." He'd been on her side even when he'd borne the brunt of her betrayal because he'd wanted the best for her and Cora.

Ivy didn't lay into him, which might mean he hadn't offended her too deeply. Maybe she'd even think about his offer to help. At the very least, he'd keep in contact with Cora and give her an outlet for her anger. Maybe he could even redirect it into positive action, though he wouldn't hold his breath. Truthfully, he'd put up a wall around his heart where Cora was concerned. With every milestone he'd missed and had to hear about second-hand, a little more of him had died. Because he still remembered her first day at kindergarten, her first lost tooth, her first crush, her first best-friend breakup, and her first stab at making his birthday cake. And so many more firsts. He treasured those memories now, blocked as he was from the rest, and the barricade he'd constructed helped keep the longing for more at bay.

Except not so much today.

"Okay. I won't get upset with her for telling you," Ivy said.

"Thanks. And my offer to help still stands if you change your mind. Just let me know."

"Goodbye, Garth." An abrupt nothingness told him Ivy had hung up.

Rising and shouldering his duffle, he went into the back door of the café. Maggie was nowhere to be seen, so he approached the two women talking with Keisha at the counter. Keisha gave him a brilliant smile. "Hi, Garth. Maggie's upstairs, so go on up."

"First you have to introduce us," said one of the new women. She had frizzy blond hair and wore a lot of makeup, which emphasized her beautiful lips. "I'm Laina, and this is Ayleen." She pointed to the other woman.

"I'm Garth. Nice to meet you."

"Are you going to be in town long?" Ayleen asked. She wore no makeup, and her straight hair was pulled back into a pony-tail. Her smile revealed perfect white teeth.

"I'm not sure yet. It depends on a few things." Cora was one of those things, but he didn't feel a need to share that with these strangers, as nice as they seemed.

"Well, I hope you stay a long time," Laina said. "We don't have any pilots around here."

"And not likely to," Keisha put in. "There's no airport and not a chance of having one, not even in Panna Creek. Not yet."

The other women sighed, and Laina's pout, in particular, made him feel a little lighter. Maggie might not want him here, but these women were more than welcoming. Maybe that was a good omen.

"See you around," he said, nodding at the women. He was

around the corner and halfway up the stairs when he heard laughter following him. Probably one of them had said something about him—something flirty, no doubt. He didn't mind. Maybe he even needed it after his lackluster welcome from Maggie.

He reached a small landing where he found Maggie waiting, but she was with the man he'd seen outside earlier. She was laughing at something he'd said, her face relaxed. Until she spotted Garth and shutters went down over her dark eyes. She said something to the man.

He nodded. "I'll leave you to it," he said, his gaze flickering over Garth. "I have calls to make, but I'll be down at seven."

"I'll need to change," she said. "And I've asked Keisha to lock up for me, but I don't know if I'll be able to leave right then. You know how it goes."

"If we miss the movie, we can always do something else." He touched Maggie on the arm in farewell and nodded again at Garth before heading through a half-open door.

Garth supposed he could be grateful they hadn't kissed because even with that simple touch, he wanted to bash his fist into the man's face.

No, he thought. He was the interloper here. It wasn't eighteen years ago, and he and Maggie had never really been a couple. All the what-ifs and should-have-beens meant nothing now. He was here to set those right—or to put the feelings to rest once and for all. The anger drained away as it always did when he considered his options. Turning emotion into calm action was what he did.

Well, unless he couldn't act, and then he withdrew his heart as he'd had to do with Cora and Ivy. Bitterness bit at his throat, but he swallowed hard against the emotion, forcing a smile.

"So, where do I go?" He gestured to his bag.

"This way." She gave him a smile that didn't reflect in her eyes before leading him down the hallway to the last room on the left. "This room has a private bath. I thought you'd like that."

"You didn't give it to your other boarder?" He was probing, and she'd probably see through him.

"Connor comes for a few days every week, and he's mostly out at the job site, so he doesn't need a private bathroom. But there's no sense in your sharing with him today, so you might as well take this room." She pushed the door open to reveal a queen-sized bed with a canopy frame and gauzy, off-white curtains tied to the canopy poles. The bed was definitely the focal point, but once he tore his eyes away from the decidedly romantic setup, he noted paintings on the walls, a chair by the desk in the corner, a television, dresser, microwave, and small fridge. *Just like any motel room,* he told himself, *only nicer.*

"Will this be okay?" Maggie asked.

"Perfect." He walked inside and set his bag on the bed. She turned to go, but he couldn't leave it like that.

"How about taking me to see that lake tonight?" he suggested.

"Sorry, I actually have a prior engagement."

"With him?" he motioned to the door.

She nodded. "He leaves tonight. We always try to get together at least one evening when he's in town."

Which by Garth's way of thinking meant four dates a month. Not impressive in his view. "What about after? We could go for a drink."

She laughed, and this time her smile was real. "This isn't Trenton, and it's not a Riverband Festival. Everything closes pretty early, except the bar, and even they lock up by eleven on weekdays."

He closed the few steps between them. "Then we'll take a walk.

We don't need a bar." He might be pushing, but he'd already made it clear why he was here. "Please, Maggie."

She stared up at him, and her lips, slightly apart, begged to be kissed, even if she didn't know it. Everything about her reminded him intensely of the girl he'd loved.

"Maybe," she said. "Let's see what the evening brings." Her eyes were on him—steady and challenging. Almost taunting. All his senses told him to close that last step, to take her in his arms, but he was no longer a youth of twenty-two, driven to immediate action. Kissing her now would be premature, and he knew her well enough that she'd call him on it. A lack of passion had never been their problem. What he needed was to understand why she had cut things off. And why, even when they had both been unavailable and involved with others, he had felt an instinctual connection to her as if their single day together meant more than every other day he had lived.

He was playing the long game.

He stepped closer, smiling internally when her dark eyes widened. Tension pulsed between them as he let his eyes wander from her eyes to her lips and then back to her eyes again.

"I'll be waiting," he said softly.

He'd been waiting for eighteen years. What were a few more hours?

CHAPTER 5

Maggie escaped from the guest room, her emotions all over the place. What had just happened with Garth? One minute, she was sure she could keep things low key between them, and the next, she'd almost stepped into his arms the way she'd done so easily as a teenager on that magical day. And why she still thought of it as magical when it had led to so much heartache, she couldn't say. It made no sense.

She should hate Garth, but she didn't. She did, however, want him to go away. Instinctively, she touched the watch underneath her blouse, the solidness of it anchoring her to reality. In a few days this would be over, and she would be free to pursue her future.

Downstairs in the café, she was surprised to find Hannah back from the school and once more dressed in her apron. "I thought you'd be preparing lessons or something," Maggie said.

Hannah laughed. "Maria has lesson plans, and I'm good for

tomorrow. I can still help after school for the time being, but you'll need help for lunch."

"No," Maggie said, shaking her head. "I know you don't want to leave me hanging, but you can't teach all day, study your lesson plans, and work here as well. Besides, what about that new husband of yours, not to mention that rambunctious puppy? It's too much."

Relief was apparent on Hannah's face. "I didn't want to leave you in the lurch."

"You're not. I always knew you were only here temporarily." When Hannah had first come to town, she'd stayed in the room upstairs, and Maggie had given her a job to offset the room costs, but with the new construction in town, her shift had become vital to the café. "Ingrid has asked for more hours, and I'll cover the lunch shift somehow." Even if she had to get up earlier.

"I can put an ad in the local paper right now," Keisha said, grabbing the tablet under the counter.

Maggie nodded. "Good idea." The paper was free, and everyone in town was used to looking at it more than any online version. "Thank you." She was grateful to have Keisha do it because she wasn't all that certain anything she wrote today would make sense. "Well, I'd better prep the mashed potatoes and put in a couple of hams."

She hurried into the kitchen before Hannah could voice the questions in her eyes. No doubt she was curious about the new boarder, but Maggie didn't want to share her past, not even with these two friends.

After the hams were cooking and the potatoes boiling, she set about making a new batch of gooey butter cake. She normally made four pans once a day, setting them in the display to the left of the other cakes when they were finished. Butter cake was better after sitting twenty-four hours, so all the employees knew to choose the older cakes from the right side of the case. They cut each pan into twelve and put a dollop of fresh whipped cream on the side. Most people used a yellow cake mix for the base, but her cake was from scratch, of course. Even so, it was simple to make, and she was comforted to lose herself in the familiar routine.

Why was Garth really here? The thought was torturing. He wanted to start a new past, but that was impossible. He didn't even know everything about their first one.

"Uh, what are you doing?"

Maggie jerked her head around to see Charlotte Bennett, Forgotten's lay midwife and her best friend. "What do you mean? I'm making my gooey butter cake."

"Well, I just watched you put in two tablespoons of baking powder, and are you sure you need a third one?" Charlotte's vivid green eyes were amused.

Maggie dropped the powder back into the tin. She always put two for the four cakes, and another one wouldn't have ruined it, but the taste might have been slightly off. "Thanks. I guess my mind's elsewhere." She mixed the batter with a little more vigor than necessary.

Charlotte wrinkled her nose that was slightly spattered with freckles. "It's about Hannah, isn't it? Why you're distracted, I mean. I'm sorry about that, but you always knew she'd be leaving. And it's a good thing for the school. If Hannah weren't here, those kids would have a string of substitutes who don't know anything about teaching."

"Yeah, I know. It might be a little rough for a few days here, but Keisha is putting in an ad for a new employee."

"I'm always willing to help out if you need me." Charlotte

leaned against the counter near Maggie. "I became quite good at it during Hannah's honeymoon."

"You really did." Maggie started pouring the batter into the pans, and Charlotte handed her a rubber spatula. Maggie smiled. "Thanks. I'm not too worried about losing Hannah. It always works out in the end."

"Because you're good at finding the right people and giving them a chance." Charlotte waited a few moments before adding, "But now that Maria has delivered, I don't have another mother due for two weeks, so in a pinch, give me a call. I can reschedule my prenatal appointments."

Maggie nearly dropped her bowl. Seeing Charlotte's shoulder-length brown hair in a single French braid—her midwife look as Maggie called it—should have reminded her to ask about the baby before now. "I should have asked. How did it go?"

"Both Maria and her baby are perfectly fine, but Maria is something else. She began feeling labor pains at lunchtime, but she stayed for another class anyway. She called me from the school, and I picked her up because she was too far into labor already to drive herself. I took her right over to the clinic. She was not happy about that, I can tell you, but we weren't going to make the fifteen minutes to her house. She barely got into a gown before she wanted to push. I had to break her water, or the baby would have come out in the sack." Charlotte gave her a weary smile. "But in the end, everything was fine. She had a boy, eight pounds. Maria's husband, her father-in-law, and uncle are over the moon to finally have an heir to their ranches. Apparently, Maria's two little girls and her sister-in-law's four girls don't count in that respect."

"They might find themselves surprised." Maggie opened one

of her industrial-sized ovens and slid two pans inside. "Still, ranching's a hard life for anyone, male or female."

The old Ramos brothers, Easton and Asher, were as alike as non-twin brothers could be. They dressed the same, had the same mannerisms, each owned their own cattle ranch, and they came in a couple of times a week to eat at the Butter Cake and make small talk with their buddies. The biggest difference between them was that Easton had never married, while Asher was a widower with two grown kids, including a son who'd married Maria.

"Ranching has its good side. Anyway, the labor was short and intense, same as with her previous children, and she was out of there as fast as her husband could drive her home. Gives a new meaning to the term drive-by delivery." Charlotte paused, studying her with a sideway tilt of her head. "But if you're not worried about losing Hannah, what has you so preoccupied? Is everything okay?"

Of course Charlotte would pick up on her angst. Maggie took a breath and put the remaining pans in the oven, lowering her voice before saying, "Not exactly."

"What? Is it Connor? Is he wanting more?" Charlotte knew Maggie was considering a relationship with him. She also knew that his being in town for only a day or two each week both attracted and concerned Maggie, who valued her autonomy.

"Not exactly." Maggie scratched the side of her nose that somehow had flour on it and looked away from Charlotte. "It's Garth. He's here."

The information took time for Charlotte to process because though Maggie had confided about meeting Garth and her short career in music, they only talked about him when Maggie opted yet again to avoid another relationship. Charlotte thought

Maggie was over-romanticizing her time with Garth—and she probably was—but Charlotte didn't know the whole story.

"You mean Garth as in Trenton and the one-night fling with the US Air Force pilot?"

"It wasn't a fling." But even as she said it, Maggie knew it couldn't be called anything else. Twenty-six hours together, talking about everything under the sun, letting passion rule her heart, and she hadn't even given him her contact information. Why? Because he was going overseas, and she knew what that meant. She wasn't one of those girls who chased a man simply because he was in uniform. She would *never* be like her mother. And four years later, after she'd seen Garth's wife and his three-year-old daughter, she knew she'd made the right choice.

Which brought her to wondering—why was he here, and why did she care?

"I assume he's here to see you," Charlotte pressed.

Maggie nodded. "He saw me singing online. And now he's here, and I . . ." She didn't know what she was.

"You think you're still in love with him."

"Shh!" Maggie hissed, though there was no way anyone two feet away could hear them, much less anyone outside the kitchen.

Charlotte regarded her calmly. "It's good that he's here. Maybe you can finally see your relationship for what it really was. Because you need to move on. We both know that. You want a family—and while thirty-six isn't too old, not in this day and age, it's pushing things. Five of the women I've helped deliver in the past three years have been over forty, and the pregnancies are always more challenging. You have to get past what you've built up in your mind about him so you can grab your dreams."

"It's not that easy." Tears came unbidden to Maggie's eyes. "I-I didn't tell you everything."

"Then maybe it's time you do." There was no surprise in Charlotte's tone. When Maggie stared at her, Charlotte nodded. "Of course I knew. Otherwise, why would you have put your entire life on hold? Why did you really leave your career right when it was finally taking off? What happened?"

Maggie touched the watch between her breasts and shook her head. "I'll tell you later. I still have to get through dinner." Without breaking down, she meant, and she would break down if she said any more. It would be too real.

Charlotte gave her arm a little squeeze. "Okay, but I'm not letting you off the hook that easy. I'll run some errands and come back. We'll talk after work."

"I can't. Connor's taking me to the movie."

Charlotte laughed. "Does Garth know about this?"

"I told him. He wants me to take him to the lake after—not going to happen." She couldn't trust herself. "But I would love it if you'd just happen to be here later, so he can't talk me into anything I'll regret."

"Is that really what you want?" Charlotte stared at her doubtfully.

"Yes. No. I don't know."

"How about I sleep over? I don't have anything to do tonight. I'll wait up in your room, and that way if you need me, I'll be here, but if you decide to go somewhere with Garth, you can do that too without me getting in the way."

"That sounds perfect." Relief flooded Maggie. "You really are my best friend."

"I know." Charlotte hugged her and waved goodbye as she left the kitchen.

Maggie turned to set the timer on her cake. She'd have to eat a piece when it was done to make sure she hadn't left out anything.

People came from nearby towns for her gooey butter cake, and she couldn't let her distraction with Garth sully the name she'd worked so hard to build.

Hannah sent back an order, and Maggie eagerly pounced on it. A special, or a little bit of everything she was serving for that particular meal, which for tonight's dinner meant steak, ham, pork, potatoes, rice, fries, a side salad, a slice of bread with butter, and a piece of gooey butter cake. She quickly threw the meat on the grill and lowered a portion of fries. As the night went on, she'd put extra meat on the grill to keep ahead, but it shouldn't be that busy for a while yet.

She was wrong about that, though. Apparently, other people in Forgotten were every bit as curious about the Air Force pilot as Laina and Ayleen had been, and word spread fast. It didn't take her long to learn that Ronica Wilson had been making the rounds and talking about the new pilot. She'd even been to see the new Ramos baby on the pretext of taking them her famous Kansas dirt cake, and the old Ramos brothers themselves had come into the café to get a "gander" at the real-life Air Force hero.

Was Garth an actual hero? She didn't know. He could be decorated a hundred times over for all she knew. Or he might be the kind who ran when confronted with danger. Did he fire first and ask questions later? No, she didn't believe that. But he could be the kind who cheated on his wife with another woman.

Stop, she told herself. She didn't know if he'd been married when they met, but when they exchanged all those romantic emails, his daughter had already been born or was about to be. Maggie pushed the thoughts away and called one of her teenage employees to help take orders so Hannah could fill plates with her in the kitchen. As she forced a smile with each plate she delivered to the front counter, she was more than grateful that Hannah had come back today.

She knew immediately when Garth finally entered the dining room because the volume in the café cut in half as people apparently stopped talking to stare at him. Gradually, though, the volume resumed, and Maggie filled another tray with plates to carry out to the front. She could have asked Hannah to take them, but she wasn't going to hide in her own café. She stepped out of the kitchen, her smile hopefully genuine as she nodded at people eating at the counter. So far, so good.

Then she spied Garth, and all the others fell away. He stood in line at the register, his head cocked upward as he read the menu. His eyes met hers, their dark blue irises intense, his square jaw firm, his face oh-so-attractive and compelling. The years peeled away, and she saw him as she first had at Trenton eighteen years ago. She'd been on stage, her voice ringing out over the crowd, and suddenly there he was, dressed in a uniform and standing slightly apart from his friends as if an unseen spotlight had zeroed in on his position and everyone else had stepped away from the light. He was staring at her. Their eyes met and held— and she'd given her singing a little more effort because she knew he'd be waiting for her afterward.

He *had* been waiting for her, but so had someone from Axel Zyon's office, and the agent had given her Axel's card. Her excitement at being approached by a talent agent had added to the thrill of finding Garth waiting.

"You're amazing," he'd said in apparent admiration.

She'd smiled. "I think I deserve ice cream. Don't you?"

"Only if I'm buying."

"What about your friends?" She looked over his shoulder at his Air Force buddies.

"No ice cream for them. I'll find my own way home."

And the marvelous, wonderful, incredible, earth-shattering—heartbreaking—day had begun.

"Hey, Maggie!" a voice cut through her memories. "Why don't you sing that song for us right now? They're saying online that you're even better than the original artist."

The voice was familiar, but Maggie couldn't put a name to it. Her gaze didn't leave Garth, though she was abruptly aware of others in the café now as she hadn't been moments before. Would he tell them the truth? A word from him might end her anonymity here in Forgotten. But Garth only nodded to her.

Maggie tore her gaze away from Garth to see Jeremy Wilson, Ronica's youngest son, at the counter, a full plate in front of him. "Sorry," she said sweetly, handing the tray of orders to Keisha. "I think people would much rather eat on time than hear me sing. No one likes burned steaks." With that, she turned and went back into the kitchen.

She continued to cook and fill plates in a sort of comforting haze. She loved the smell, the repetition, creating the dishes, her kitchen. This was her domain, and it was safe—her happy place. Why then did her thoughts keep going back to Garth and what she was going to tell him when the time finally came?

CHAPTER 6

Eventually, the orders ceased, and they turned the closed sign over on the door. They always closed at seven because no one really came after that. The movie theater started shortly after, and most other places were already closed. Farmers and ranchers needed to tend their animals and go to bed to get up early. On the weekends, the café stayed open until nine, but not many came in after eight, unless it was a special occasion.

Outside at the counter, and to Maggie's relief, Garth was nowhere to be seen. She left Keisha to close up, and she hurried upstairs to change from her jeans and white blouse to a loose navy dress with cap sleeves. It was casual enough for a movie but dressy enough to match the dress pants and polo Connor would likely be wearing.

Connor was waiting downstairs when she descended, and they hurried out to his gray sedan together, even though the theater was just down the street, so they wouldn't be late. The opening commercials were still playing as they walked into the theater with a tub of popcorn and two drinks. Maggie nodded at the few clumps of people as they moved down the aisle. The movie had been in town three weeks already, so there weren't more than thirty people in the theater. No one seemed to be paying much attention to Maggie and Connor, but people would notice their presence, and since it wasn't the first time they'd been out together, some might assume they were more than casually dating. Maybe she didn't care. Maybe it was time. Connor was an attractive, successful man, and she liked him. A lot.

The movie started off with a chase scene, and Maggie tried to immerse herself in the plot. Darkness wrapped around her like a soft blanket of obscurity. She barely noticed when Connor's arm stretched over the back of her chair. What was Garth doing now? There wasn't much to do in Forgotten, so he was probably in his room. Or could he even now be in the theater somewhere? Her body tensed at the thought, and she lost track of the rest of the movie.

She blinked in surprise as the ending credits began rolling and the lights went on. Connor grinned at her, and she smiled back. "Not bad," he said.

"Yeah." She craned her neck, looking around at the scattering people. No sign of Garth.

"Looking for someone?"

"Not really."

They headed out to the car, where he opened the door for her. "They're making really good progress on the factory," he said as he started the engine. "They might be able to start production as soon as eight more months. They'll be hiring nearly a hundred people before then."

"What about the housing development?" A hundred workers

would mean families moving in and more business for all of Forgotten.

"They've already started building a dozen houses, and the company will lease those out to the managers until they buy their own. By the time the factory is ready, there will be enough for the workers to lease or buy as well." He grinned. "Or for people here in Forgotten to trade up and sell their old ones to the new workers. You think you might want one?"

She laughed. "I'm happy with the house I've got."

"It's a beautiful house." As he spoke, his warm eyes fixed on her.

"Guess we'll have to change the population sign," she said.

He chuckled and finally started the car moving. Silence fell during the two-minute drive to her café. "You still driving back to Lincoln tonight?" she asked as he pulled into her parking lot. "Because you don't have to." She could have kicked herself for saying it. She needed to deal with Garth, and it would be easier without Connor around.

"I've got an important meeting in the morning, and I've already put my things in the trunk. Come on. I'll walk you in."

They walked up the side path, where they both stopped at the back door to the café. Maggie would make the rounds on the main floor before she went to bed, mostly checking lights, tomorrow's food prep, and double-checking the locks on the doors. There wasn't much crime in Forgotten, and many people didn't lock their doors, but she always did—a lesson learned on the road during her short career.

The chestnut color of his skin looked darker under the moonlight. Keisha had forgotten to turn on the lights in the back, which Maggie usually left on, but maybe it was better this way. She was all too aware that Garth was somewhere in her café, or maybe taking a walk. She didn't want questions from him about Connor.

"You seem a million miles away tonight," Connor said. "Is something bothering you? Or did I offend you in some way?"

Maggie's stomach sank. "No. I'm sorry. I do have some things on my mind, but it's nothing to do with you." Her response sounded almost as bad, as if she were telling him he had no input in the part of her life that was causing her stress—which didn't say much for their relationship.

Connor didn't take offense. "Is it your other boarder? You seemed a little upset in the café when he was there for dinner."

"Café?" Maggie repeated stupidly. Connor had been there? She hadn't even noticed. "Did I act strange?" Had the whole town picked up on her reaction to Garth? Her reputation meant a lot to her—the reputation she'd worked hard to build. His presence endangered that.

"Not so much that anyone would notice," Connor said, a smile coming to his face. "I always pay attention to you." The amusement in his voice made the comment teasing. "Plus, there seemed to be some tension between you two this afternoon when we were talking upstairs." He jerked his head, indicating the second floor.

"Well, there is a little tension. I met him in Canada as a girl. Just briefly. It was a surprise to see him here."

Connor's smile faded. "All the way from Canada, huh? That's a strange coincidence. Unless you invited him, of course."

"He's not from Canada. He was there for some joint Air Force venture between Canada and the US. Apparently, he saw me singing online and decided to look me up."

"You think he's stalking you?" Connor's voice was tense now.

"No. Oh, no. Definitely not. It's not like that." No way could she possibly explain Garth to him.

"Are you sure? Because I can ask him to leave—if you want."

Maggie wouldn't want to see the end of that confrontation. Connor was fit and muscular, but he was no fighter. Garth was a trained military man and stood a good three inches taller. "It's really fine. I'm glad to have the chance to catch up with him. I sang once at his base when he was stationed in Texas."

"Sang?"

Too late, she remembered that while she had told Connor about growing up in Canada, and even about her mother, she hadn't told him about her brief career.

She shrugged. "I did a little singing when I first moved to America. Not a big deal."

Connor stepped closer to her. "Well, you're good at it. I saw the recording too."

"Really?" He didn't seem the type of person to spend a lot of time online.

"Three different people here showed it to me." His voice was lower now, and he had that look in his eyes that told her he was going to kiss her. Normally, she would have welcomed his kiss, and it certainly wouldn't be the first time, but tonight it felt as if eyes were everywhere.

Or at least one certain pair of eyes. She mentally cursed herself for her stupidity, and Garth as well. Why couldn't he leave the past where it belonged? Still, it wasn't Garth she wished would leave right now, but Connor.

His gaze holding hers, Connor moved closer, clearly misinterpreting her signals. He was a handsome man—she'd always thought so—but tonight having him this close made her anxious. And why? Because of Garth.

That thought spurred her forward to meet Connor's kiss. Her arms went up around his neck. He smelled like aftershave, and the trim hair on his face tickled her nose. Why had she never noted that before? Then she felt his lips more firmly against hers as his arms tightened. That was more like it.

She let herself melt into him. He was a good, kind man. Yes, he didn't know about her past, but did it really matter? She didn't think so. He'd been poor as a child, growing up in a rough area of town as a minority, but he had worked hard to get where he was today. He'd understand where she'd come from.

The kiss deepened, and Connor's breath came faster. Unbidden, Garth's face popped into her mind. Not his face when they'd first met but the older Garth, the man who'd finally come looking for her.

Finally?

She broke away. "You've got a long drive to Lincoln," she said. "And I'd better check the café. Thank you so much for a nice evening."

He nodded. "I'll call you. I was thinking maybe you'd enjoy a weekend away in Lincoln sometime, or I could come back here a day early. I still want to try out the lake for fishing."

"Maybe this weekend?" Would Garth be gone by then? Yes. She couldn't live like this that long.

"Still need to check my schedule," he said.

"Let's text then," she said. Guilt assaulted her because right that moment, she would say anything to get him to leave. She needed to think.

"Will do." With a nod and a smile, Connor headed to the parking lot.

"I'm sorry," Maggie whispered, watching him go. Were things not working out between them because they weren't right together or because Garth was here?

She simply didn't know.

Letting herself into the café, Maggie carefully closed and

locked the door behind her. As she started forward in the café, lit only partially by the perfectly spaced nightlights she'd installed in the walls, a figure suddenly loomed in front of her. Her heart leapt into a furious pounding, and she wished she hadn't left her gun upstairs in her room. Before she could say anything or reach for her keys to thread between her fingers, a light went on in the computer room. There stood Garth, now framed in the light, his arm falling back to his side.

"Hey," he said. "Sorry if I scared you. I was using the computer and didn't want to, uh, disturb you, so I used the flashlight on my phone instead of turning on the light. You seemed pretty busy out there."

He'd seen her and Connor? But of course he had. "You were watching me?" she asked, her face hot.

"Not at all. I came downstairs to use the computer, and I saw you through the door. Don't worry. It was only briefly as I went in. Is that guy your boyfriend?" A slight mocking colored his tone.

Anger swept through her. It was because of him that her insides twisted and her emotions were in shambles. Because of him she couldn't even enjoy a movie and the goodnight kiss of a man she cared about.

"Does it matter?" she asked.

"Well, yes." He was serious now. "Otherwise, building a new past might be kind of hard."

"You know it's not going to be that kind of past, don't you?"

"I don't know anything yet. That's why I'm here." He kept his gaze on hers, and she looked away first. "Could we go for a walk?" he asked.

"I need to check the café first."

"Okay. I'll wait." He sat down at the nearest table and pulled out his cell phone.

Maggie gave herself over to habit as she went through her mental checklist. Everything looked wiped down, from the windowsills to the desk in the computer room. Her newly baked butter cakes—which had miraculously turned out perfect—were now cooled and in their proper spot in the display or in the refrigerator where she stored the extras. The meats for tomorrow were marinating, and the ingredients for tomorrow's spinach soup were prechopped. The lights in front and the outside café sign were on, but the closed sign had been placed on both doors, which were locked. She checked the garage and the kitchen door that led to the outside tables, also all locked. There was nothing more to do.

She slid into the seat across from him, exhaustion spreading through her. She doubted she would ever be able to move again. "I'm actually a little tired, so maybe we can do this tomorrow? I was up early and will have to be in the morning as well."

His forehead wrinkled in concern. "I should have thought of that. Just because I'm here between jobs doesn't mean your life stops. How can I help?"

He looked so earnest sitting there, his face mostly shadowed except for the light still coming from the open door of the computer room. He looked younger, more like the boy she'd willingly stayed up all night with at their very first meeting. She still remembered vividly how they'd danced for hours in the streets, played fair games, taken a boat ride, made out all the way through a movie, and watched the sunrise before eating donuts and finding a place to crash in each other's arms. Sleep hadn't seemed to matter. Only being together had been important that day—no, not just important but vital to her existence.

That, however, had been looking through the lens of youth, and she no longer had the inexperience that luxury required.

"You can't really help. It's just food prep." Since Hannah would be at the school now, she'd have to do breakfast alone, which probably wouldn't be too terrible. She'd done it for months before Hannah's arrival in town. "But afternoons are slow, so I can usually take time off then, or tomorrow night." Something niggled inside her head at the statement, but she couldn't connect it with anything at the moment. She'd have to check her calendar to see if there was a conflict.

"It's a date then."

She didn't protest, though it wasn't really a date.

His hand went over hers where it rested on the table. "Is everything else okay?"

How to answer that? Nothing was okay or could be okay until she resolved their past, and while she was angry at him for being here, she was also glad that he was. She needed to tell him the truth.

"You can tell me anything, you know."

That made her smile. "You said that once before."

His boyish chuckle took her by surprise. "You remember."

"Yes." She remembered everything that happened that day. Unfortunately, it always ended the same way—with unimaginable heartache.

"Me too." His thumb massaged hers ever-so-gently, his skin slightly rough. "Every second. That day sometimes seems more real to me than all the others I've lived before and most after. I used to think of it when I flew into combat. It . . . it represented what I was fighting for."

She understood what he meant because the memory had been the only thing keeping her alive during those terrible years that followed. Even sometimes now, she remembered it when she thought about giving up on love. But why did he recall their day and not the day he'd married his wife or the day his daughter had come into the world?

"I know it might sound odd," he said, his voice coming out huskily. "But I've missed you."

The old longing stirred inside her. His intense gaze was every bit as tangible to her as his touch on her hand. When he looked at her like that, she wanted him. Wanted him more than she'd ever wanted anyone—which had been the problem for the past eighteen years. He was a phantom lover, a man too perfect for other men to compete with. Good men like Connor.

She wanted to challenge Garth, to ask him why he felt he had the right to speak to her that way. Not after all she'd been through.

None of which he knew, of course. Which meant she was the one being unfair.

"Just tell me one thing," he asked softly. "Why did you stop emailing? Was it your agent? Were you together even then? Or heading that way?"

"No," she managed. "I just . . . I don't know." It was a lie—could he tell?

"Maggie," he whispered, his voice aggrieved.

Yes, he knew it was a lie, and the real answer to his question was why he'd come. She'd known it from the moment she'd seen him. They'd had a once-in-a-lifetime connection, one that shouldn't have ended but somehow had. She blamed herself more than him. At least, she blamed herself now; she couldn't blame the child she'd been. Would there be a way to explain to him without making him hate her?

She took a steadying breath. "I need to get some sleep." She needed to fall in bed and erase this entire day. He nodded, slid his hand away from hers, and stood. At once she felt bereft, as if she'd lost something she could never, ever replace.

She rose as well, her heart thudding dully inside her chest. *Go,* she told herself. But she didn't. She stood facing him, eyes locked. Why didn't he move aside?

"Goodnight, Maggie," he said, his voice low and incredibly compelling. He bent toward her.

Maybe he'd meant to offer a casual kiss on the cheek between old friends. Or maybe he'd meant to give her a hug. Whatever his original intention, their lips somehow found each other, and all the passion she'd bottled up inside ignited, shattering her barriers. Her mouth opened to his, tasting heat and musk and something all his own. With a little groan, his hand went around her back, pulling her toward him at the same time he stepped forward.

Maggie was flying. Everything dropped away except his touch, his taste, his smell. This was what she remembered, this magic, this moment that existed only in his arms. They were one, molded together in soul and in need. His kiss trailed down her neck, leaving a path of flames and heat and desire. Had anything ever felt so right?

His mouth found hers again, and for an endless moment Maggie was completely lost in their kiss. She'd felt exactly like this on the day they met. Why had she ever let him go? She wanted to weep and cling to him more tightly. She wanted to scream out her secrets. She wanted the moment to never end.

When he drew away at last—and it was him because she was helpless to do so—his blue eyes seemed almost black and full of need. The slightest of smiles curved his lips. "I'm glad you still remember how it was between us," he said.

"Is that what this is about?" she asked, deflated. "You're trying to prove something because you saw me kiss Connor?"

"You kissed him?" His chuckle was mocking. "Is *that* what you call it?"

She couldn't respond because he was right. It had been nice and comfortable, but she hadn't been present in the moment. She hadn't felt anything close to the way she had just now. Connor never made her feel that way.

"This isn't about anyone but you and me," Garth said into the silence. "It's about what you still feel for me and what I never stopped feeling for you."

Maggie pushed past him. "I have to go to bed." She left him there in the half darkness, her feet pounding up the stairs to the second floor. She didn't stop running until she'd closed the door to her suite behind her, letting her forehead rest against the wood.

Was she completely crazy? Why had she kissed him? It would only make it more difficult to walk away—again.

And what if she didn't have to walk away?

Except that could never be. The girl she'd been made that decision, not once but three times, and there was no going back despite Garth's talk about building a new past. There was only one past, and hers was littered with decisions that had seemed the only one possible at the time but now seemed to make little sense. Especially when Garth kissed her.

"Maggie?"

She started at the soft voice, turning around to see her best friend Charlotte standing in her sitting room, her face wrinkled with concern.

"Oh," Maggie said, bringing a hand to her suddenly racing heart—and feeling the pocket watch under her dress. "You scared me."

Charlotte grinned. "You forgot I was coming? Well, in that case, I'm glad you and your pilot friend didn't decide to come here to talk."

"Oh, no." The last thing she needed was to be in her room with Garth. Not after a single kiss had her knees melting. Maggie dropped her hand from the watch. "I'm sorry about making you come here. I really am okay."

"Are you kidding? After what you didn't tell me in the kitchen earlier? I'm dying to know what happened. I've been worrying ever since we talked. And looking at you, I'm glad I came. Come here. You look like you need a hug." She opened her arms, and Maggie stepped into them.

"It's all a mess," Maggie murmured, feeling close to tears. "Why don't we understand that the choices we make when we're barely more than kids will affect our entire lives?"

Charlotte patted her back. "Yeah, I'm with you on that. But you are the strongest woman I know. Tell me what happened, and we'll figure this out together. You are not alone."

Maggie choked back a sob. "Okay."

They sat on the couch together, Maggie bringing out her pocket watch to hold it tightly in her hands. "I didn't just meet Garth and fall in love with him eighteen years ago. I . . . we also had a son."

CHAPTER 7

Garth watched Maggie go without another word, knowing it was the best thing for now, but also because he felt rooted to the floor in shock. He *had* been trying to make a point with the kiss—mostly because seeing her with her date had evoked a jealousy he had no right to feel—but that had backfired because he'd been the one who hadn't wanted to let her go. He'd been blown away by the taste and touch and smell of her.

After all this time, he hadn't expected to feel the exact same connection he'd felt on that first day with Maggie. He was more experienced now, more jaded. But holding her was every bit as powerful now as it had been when he was twenty-two. From the moment their eyes had locked when she'd been on stage to the moment he'd brushed a tear from her cheek before kissing her goodbye, he'd ridden a wave of . . . well, euphoria. There was no other way to describe it. Over the years, he'd told himself the emotions had been amplified by time and his impending departure overseas. But here he was, forty years old and not going anywhere—and it was real. But something had gone wrong along the way, and he needed to find out what. Even if it meant finally and forever being able to say goodbye.

The thought depressed him, so he pushed it aside. He'd fight this time. All he had was time.

Sighing, he went back up to his room, which he'd left unlocked, pausing in the hallway. Were those voices coming from Maggie's room? He listened but heard nothing more, so it was probably in his imagination. Fighting the urge to pound on her door to demand answers, he reached for his own doorknob instead. How could he convince her to talk to him when she obviously hadn't been willing to confide in him before?

He had barely pulled off his shirt to change when his phone buzzed. The caller ID told him it was Ivy. That was odd. Maybe she'd changed her mind about his help with a car for Cora.

"Hello?" He sat on the bed, his hand going absently to the scar that ran diagonally across his chest from the middle of his right clavicle to his sternum. Skin grafts had done wonders to repair the damage from the plane crash when he'd been shot down during his last tour in Afghanistan, and massage, eating right, and time had eased the tightness of the grafts. But he still found himself tracing the rough pattern more than he would like to admit.

"Do you know where she is?" Ivy demanded. "Did you help her do this?"

"Whoa, slow down. Are you talking about Cora?"

"Of course I'm talking about Cora. She's missing! I can't find her anywhere. Her phone goes right to voicemail, and she's not at her friends or her dad's."

The reference to Cora's father shouldn't sting, but it did. Garth began pacing. "Did she take anything with her? A suitcase? A backpack? I'm assuming your car is still there?"

"Yes, the car's here. Just a minute." There was a pause and something that sounded like a closet opening. "Suitcases are here too." Another pause. "There are two backpacks here, but I got her a new one, and that's gone."

"She take any clothes?"

"I don't know." Ivy blew out an exasperated breath. "She's a teenager. She's got a whole closet full of clothes, half of which she never wears. How am I supposed to tell if anything is missing?"

"Shoes then."

"Um . . . yes, her new tennis shoes are gone, and her favorite sandals."

"Does she have a boyfriend?"

"No," Ivy snapped. "We just moved here. There hasn't been time."

"He might not be from there." Cora was upset about leaving, after all. A boy could be involved.

"I've called all her friends and their parents. Everyone claims they haven't seen or heard from her."

"Then maybe it's time to call the police."

"And tell them what? That we had a fight? Do you really think they'll look for her?"

"You need to get it on their radar." Now probably wasn't the time to remind her that hundreds of thousands of children went missing every year in the US alone. He'd seen for himself the depravities exploited children suffered on foreign soil, and he knew from his brief intelligence missions that it was every bit as bad in the Land of the Free. "Ivy, listen to me. Please report it. She's smart, but she's too young to be out there alone." The idea of Cora being picked up by human traffickers made him crazy.

"Okay." Ivy sounded scared now instead of angry. "I'll do that. But you'd better call me if she contacts you. Promise?"

"Of course. I promise." He'd never broken a promise to her that wasn't related to his military orders, and he'd always done everything to help Cora, even from the start. In fact, he now believed she was the reason he'd married Ivy so quickly. Maybe if he hadn't, he could have saved them all pain.

"Okay. Thanks." The line went dead.

Garth stared at the phone in his hand for a moment before calling Cora himself. When the message clicked on immediately, he knew the phone was off. "Cora, it's Garth," he said. "Please call me. I've been talking with your mother. Let's try to work things out, okay? Your mother loves you, and you've made your point. Please, we need to know you're safe."

That was all he could do, but it didn't mean he was happy. After absent-mindedly brushing his teeth, he called Cora again before finally dropping into bed. He was exhausted, both emotionally and physically.

He'd barely drifted off when he began to dream of Cora flying a fighter jet into combat, and he awoke in a sweat. It was going to be a long night.

CHAPTER 8

"**A** son," Charlotte said, her expression sympathetic. "Wow. That's huge."

"I know." Maggie's voice was scarcely a whisper. Because that was only the beginning of what she'd lived through.

Charlotte laid a hand on her shoulder. "Look, it's clear you need to lie down, so why don't you go get ready for bed? I'll get us a snack and meet you in your room. You don't have to tell me tonight if you don't want to, but I think you'll be happier if you do. Go on."

Maggie was relieved to have time to visit the bathroom and change. As she splashed water over her face, she realized Charlotte had given her a way to back out of their pending conversation. She didn't need to spill her guts tonight or ever.

Except she did. Garth was here, obviously as stuck as she was in the past, and talking to Charlotte would be good practice for when she told him. The big difference was that Charlotte would still be her friend after she was finished, and Garth?

Well, he'd likely be out of here faster than he could start up his rental car.

All for the best, she thought, then flushed as she remembered her response to his kiss. No wonder she was single—she really was still hung up on Garth.

Charlotte was waiting cross-legged on her bed with a tray carrying two huge bowls of mint chocolate chip ice cream. Maggie, now in her nightshirt, padded over to her bed, set her pocket watch on the nightstand, and tucked her bare legs under the sheets before reaching for one of the bowls. It wasn't until she took a bite and the sweetness hit her tastebuds that she remembered she'd already eaten ice cream today. Her heart squeezed painfully.

"You don't like it? I thought it was your favorite."

"I-I had some today . . . with Garth." The last two words were almost unintelligible.

"Oh, sweetie." Charlotte scooted closer, taking the bowl from her. "That's okay."

Maggie grabbed the bowl back. "I still want it." Who wouldn't? She leaned back on the pillows, setting the bowl on her chest. She spooned another huge mound of ice cream into her mouth.

"Okay then." Charlotte chuckled and picked up her own bowl, also stretching out on the bed next to her, their shoulders barely brushing.

Maggie ate ice cream as if it were the only thing holding her to sanity. She'd spent extra for this brand, with extra large chunks of chocolate and thick, creamy mint that sent happy vibes throughout her body. No wonder she loved it so much.

It absolutely wasn't because it reminded her of Garth and falling in love.

"So, do you want to talk?" Charlotte asked, staring up at the ceiling as if the swirled pattern entranced her.

The swirls reminded Maggie of clouds, and she studied the ceiling, letting her spoon rest in the bowl. Half the ice cream was already gone. "I don't know where to begin."

"Well, I know about the day you met and how he wanted your contact information but you refused."

"I didn't want to be like my mother, you know?" Maggie frowned. "And yet I was exactly like her."

"Because you got pregnant like she did? That doesn't mean you were the same."

"It meant I was a stupid kid. What was I thinking? That just because Garth seemed like a dream, nothing bad would happen? Of course it wouldn't work out."

"Don't be so hard on yourself. We all did stupid things when we were young. You can't change the past. It's who you've become now that is important."

Maggie stared again at the white ceiling. "You're right. And God knows I paid the price."

Charlotte nodded but didn't speak. She simply waited as Maggie ate more ice cream. Eventually, the treat was gone, and there was nothing left but the story.

"I told you about Garth, but what I didn't tell you was the next morning, before he left, he asked me to marry him."

"He asked you to marry him after only a day?"

Maggie nodded, peeking at Charlotte to see her mouth agape. "Yes, but it didn't feel like that. It felt like . . ." Like she'd known him forever. She would never forget his exact words because they felt like her own, even then, before she'd written the song.

"This feeling for you takes me by surprise, Maggie Tremblay," he'd said. "As if there's no beginning and no end. It's just you and me."

Maggie shut her heart against the memory. "Of course, he didn't have a ring, so he gave me this." She twisted to her side, leaning over to place the empty bowl on her nightstand and grabbing her pocket watch, the chain tinkling against the outside of the ice cream bowl. "I didn't know it at the time, but it's gold."

"I admit, I've wondered where you got it."

Maggie knew because Charlotte had asked at least twice when Maggie checked the time, and she'd always said from an old friend. It hadn't exactly been a lie.

"Of course I told him his proposal was ridiculous, that we'd just met."

"It *was* ridiculous."

Was it wrong that Maggie still wished she'd said yes? Her father might have stayed with her mother for several years, but he'd never proposed.

"On the wharf where we said goodbye, he still made me keep the watch," Maggie said. "He promised he was going to find me, even though I refused to give him my address or phone number."

"Because of what happened between your mother and father?"

"That's what I told myself then." Maggie sighed. "Maybe I was scared. It's a big leap, falling in love."

"So you kept the watch and thought that was the end of it. What about the baby? What happened there?"

"Well, before I knew about the baby, I was offered a contract to sing," she began. "It was a once in a lifetime opportunity, and when I found out I was pregnant, it was like I'd ruined everything. My mother, the agency—everyone—wanted me to get an abortion. Everyone but my neighbor, Delitra. She's the lady I often helped stuff envelopes in her kitchen after school when I was a kid. That was her job, and I'd go over there when my mother was at work . . . or drunk. She'd been trying to have a baby for years, and she told me what a miracle it was. She was excited for me, even under the circumstances."

Charlotte's spoon clinked into her empty bowl. "And how did you feel about it?"

"That's what was so strange. Even though I had a terrible childhood, I was glad to be alive, and I felt my baby deserved the same chance. And plus . . ." She met Charlotte's gaze. "Maybe there was a part of me that wanted Garth's child. For a few months, I even imagined he would somehow find out and come back for me and that . . . I don't know." She waited a few seconds before adding, "The song, my big hit single? Well, it was inspired by what he said to me when he proposed. I guess somehow I thought he'd hear it and understand the message, but my agent insisted it was too depressing, so I only performed it live in bars. It didn't make the cut to the recording studio until a year later." She'd eventually added the third, more positive verse to make that happen, the verse she thought of as her son's.

"Did you try to find him?"

"No. I was too proud. Then my career started taking off, despite the pregnancy. The agency still wanted me, if I could figure out childcare, but it didn't take me long to realize I had no way to raise the baby. We were on the road a lot, even then, singing in bars and restaurants, staying at cockroach motels, and selling singles—all the while trying to write more songs. That's no life for a child, and my mother . . . well, I knew firsthand how unstable she was."

"Soooo, did you . . .?" There was a touch of horror on Charlotte's face.

"No. Of course not." Maggie was happy to put her mind at ease. "I decided to place him for adoption." She paused and gave a humorless laugh. "That sounds far easier than it was."

"I can imagine." Charlotte's hand grabbed hers and squeezed.

"I went into labor a month early. My placenta separated from my uterus, and I almost lost him."

Charlotte nodded. "I suspected something like that when you helped me with Hannah when she had her issues. So he survived?"

"Yes, and I had him for two weeks all to myself in a motel in Tennessee. That was how long it took to work out everything for Delitra to come and get Zach."

A little sound escaped Charlotte's mouth. "Oh, your friend."

"I wanted someone I knew would love him. But giving him up after those weeks . . ." Tears dripped down Maggie's face. "I don't know how I did it, but it was for him." She clicked open the pocket watch to reveal not only a timepiece in the bottom portion, but a picture of her son nestled inside the top cover.

"A handsome boy," Charlotte said, turning on her side, her head propped up on her bent elbow and hand. "Was his name your choice?"

"Delitra and I decided together before he was born. Her husband was so thrilled to have a son that we could have named him Zebediah if we wanted, which was a little joke between the three of us."

"You got to see him after the adoption?"

"Oh, yeah. It was so nice in the first year coming back from tour and being able to spend time with him, so I could see he was okay. Even after they moved out of Trenton, and I was permanently in the States, I'd visit occasionally, and she'd send me photographs." Maggie had scanned in and organized the pictures, which she'd had professionally printed into a beautiful, three-hundred-page memory book she'd never shown to anyone. "It made me happy, seeing him grow up, and reading Delitra's letters about him."

"You made them happy."

"For a while."

"What do you mean for a while? Did you tell Garth?"

"I almost did a few years later, but not then."

"What about those emails you told me you exchanged with him? Where does that fit in?"

Maggie clicked the watch shut and held it tightly in her hand against her heart, once again staring up at the ceiling. "Garth did track me down, but Zach was already four months old by then. For a while, I thought maybe . . ." Maggie trailed off. "It doesn't matter what I thought. There could be no future with Garth without Zach, and there was no way I was going to let my son grow up like I had—with a mother who couldn't care for him and a father who would likely abandon him. Even if Garth had been the real thing, I knew he'd never forgive me for not telling him. Plus, I didn't want to hurt Delitra if he or his family decided to go after Zach." She gave a self-deprecatory smirk. "I knew everything back then, and it made sense to me. The truth is, I think I was mad at him for taking so long. I guess I was punishing him." And herself.

"That's understandable. You went through so much all alone."

"There's more." Far, far more. Maggie's throat tasted like bile. When Charlotte's silence urged her on, she continued. "I broke off the emails with him after a couple of months and threw myself into work. My song had finally hit all the top charts, so it was the best thing I could do for my career anyway. The next time I saw Garth, Zach was already three and a half, and I'd just released my third album."

Charlotte sat up. "You saw Garth again? You never told me that." She held up a hand as Maggie looked at her. "No, it's okay. I understand why. But did he call you, or did you call him?"

"He reached out through my agent, Axel Zyon, and asked me to come to Texas and sing at his base. Apparently, he was home from Afghanistan. I thought it would be a good time to tell him about Zach . . . and his leukemia."

Charlotte gasped. "Oh, no!"

Maggie closed her eyes momentarily, blinking back new tears, then stared at the ceiling again. "Before his third birthday, Zach started getting bruises and was tired all the time. He was diagnosed with acute myeloid leukemia. Nothing they did worked to help him. I was a match, so I was planning on donating bone marrow after the chemo, but he wasn't responding to anything. I thought . . . well, I thought Garth should have a chance to see him before . . . before it was too late."

"So what did he say?"

"I never told him. Seeing him was like . . . stepping back into time. All the old feelings came rushing back, and I could tell he felt the same way—it surprised him as much as it did me. But then he introduced me to his wife and their three-year-old daughter." Maggie made her voice hard. "That little girl—that healthy little girl was only six months younger than Zach, which meant she was born right around the time I stopped emailing him."

"The jerk!"

Gratitude at her friend's indignance spurred Maggie on. "My thoughts exactly, so at his base I sang when I had to—but not *our* song—and the rest of the time I clung to Axel, who I was thinking about marrying at the time. I didn't tell Garth anything. He didn't deserve to know about Zach or participate in his . . ." *Death.* She couldn't say the word.

"But you never married Axel."

"It wouldn't have been fair to him. After the bone marrow transplant failed and Zach was gone, I didn't feel like singing anymore. So I found this place, and here I am." More tears flooded her, and Maggie cried as Charlotte gathered her into her arms, patting her back and murmuring comforting words. It helped having her there.

"I tried to give Delitra what she wanted most," Maggie hiccupped through her sobs, "but all I did was hurt her."

"Shush." Charlotte sat up and put her arms around Maggie. "You couldn't have known, and I bet she was still grateful."

"She said being Zach's mother was the best four years of her life. But I still . . ." Maggie shook her head because she didn't even know how to say the words. She should have been the one to hold his hand every night. To read him stories. To suffer alone. Logically, it wasn't fair to herself, but logic didn't enter into it. She would always be guilty.

Maggie covered her mouth with her hand to hold back tears. "I don't know if I can go through this again."

"So why is he here?" Charlotte's voice was defensive on her behalf. "You can send him packing any time you want. Or I will."

"He wants to know why I stopped emailing him."

"Tell him it's because he's a two-timing jerk." Charlotte tucked a strand of Maggie's hair behind her ear. "You don't owe him anything else." She paused before whispering, "You certainly don't owe him Zach."

Maggie blinked, and a new set of tears rolled from her eyes. She let her head rest on Charlotte's chest. "I know. But I think . . . I think maybe I need him to know."

Charlotte considered that for a moment. "I guess I understand, and maybe . . . well, there's so much you didn't tell him. Could there be things he hasn't told you? I mean, maybe he was separated at the time."

"Seems unlikely." But Maggie didn't really know. One thing was clear: Garth was here and there was still something strong between them. Maybe if she knew for sure what had been going through his mind at the time, she could better come to terms with the past.

She drew away from Charlotte, pulling her knees to her chest and wrapping her arms around them. "Do you want to see Zach's pictures?"

Charlotte's eyes filled with tears. "Yes. I do. I want to see them all."

CHAPTER 9

The next morning, Maggie had bread rising a little after five-thirty. In the warm kitchen, the loaves would be baking in an hour or so, which would fill the café with a delicious fresh-bread aroma. She would use yesterday's bread for the first few customers, but after it was toasted, it wouldn't taste that different, and the new bread would be finished soon enough.

Her mouth watered as she slathered butter on a piece of toast for her own breakfast. She felt ravenous. If she wasn't careful, all this bread and ice cream binging would make her put on weight, but without Hannah here this morning, she was going to need all the calories she could get.

She fried three slices of bacon in a pan, dumped out the excess fat, and then scrambled two eggs in the remaining juices. She was setting it out on a plate when a clearing throat made her turn.

"Oh," she said, seeing Garth standing in the doorway. He was wearing a white T-shirt and camouflage pants that somehow looked perfect on him. He'd definitely gained muscle since she'd last seen him, especially in his chest and arms. "I didn't expect you up this early. We don't even open until seven."

He grinned. "Yeah. I keep telling my body to sleep in, but twenty years of rolling out of bed early seems to be a hard habit to break. But I can wait until seven for breakfast."

"No," she said, putting the plate on the small square table she kept in the kitchen for employee breaks. "I've got food ready right here."

"Isn't that yours?"

"I'll make more. Sit." To her relief, he obeyed. She popped two thick slabs of bread in her toaster before sliding six more slices of bacon into the pan. "Butter?" she asked when the toast popped up. She felt she should know if he liked butter, but she didn't.

"Yes, please."

She spread a healthy layer from the pound she always left out on the counter, made from fresh cream Ronica Wilson brought her twice a week. "Did you sleep well?" She put the bread on a plate and slid it next to him before turning the bacon.

"Like a log, actually. That's a good mattress you've got up there."

"You were probably tired after your long drive." She turned over the sizzling bacon and started beating the eggs—half a dozen this time.

"I was." A crease appeared between his eyes as if there was something he was holding back.

"But something happened," she prompted.

He stared at her. "How do you know?"

"I'm good at reading people. Goes with the job." She tried to keep her voice light.

He sighed. "It's Ivy, my ex-wife. She called me last night to tell me Cora ran away. I keep wondering if I should go to Missouri to help look for her or something."

Of course you should, Maggie wanted to say. She removed the bacon and poured in the eggs, banging the empty bowl into the sink loudly. "And are you going?"

"I don't know. Ivy is really protective of Cora where I'm concerned. It's like she thinks I'm going to run off with her or something."

"So what else can you do?"

"I'll call Cora in a bit. I called and texted already, but she hasn't answered." His hand rubbed along his jaw, which she noticed he hadn't shaved yet today. She wondered what his face would feel like now against her own.

Stop, she told herself.

"I do have some buddies stationed at Whiteman," he added. "They might be able to pull a few strings with the local police. Problem is, I'm not sure where to have them begin looking. Ivy divorced her most recent husband, so she moved again, which is why Cora is upset. It's her last year of high school."

"That's tough. No kid should have to move her last year."

"That's what I think. Cora called me yesterday, very upset, which is the first I heard of it, so I'm trying to see if we can work something out."

His obvious concern soothed Maggie's indignation that he wasn't already on his way to Missouri to look for his daughter.

"She's probably hiding out at a friend's," Maggie said. "Teens do that a lot." Or they came to her café. She'd called more than one mom or dad when that happened, and often she'd let the kid stay the night, as long as they worked hard in the café while they were there, which somehow seemed to help the entire situation. They were always happy to talk to their parents sooner or later.

The eggs were ready, so she put them on the plate with the bacon and took them to the table, along with an empty plate for herself. "There's plenty here, if you want more." Maggie served herself half the plate before pushing it over to him. "I don't eat more than this, so the rest is for you. Would you like juice?"

"Milk, if you have it."

That's right. She remembered now how he loved milk and drank it every morning despite teasing from his fellow pilots. Apparently, it was a habit he hadn't given up. "Fresh yesterday from a local cow," she said, going to her industrial-sized refrigerator. "Organic and everything, if you're into that." She also gave him one of the mini fruit bowls she had ready for the breakfast rush.

He chuckled. "Guess that's one advantage of living in a small farming town. Shorter supply route."

She filled a glass of water from the sink for herself. "Yep, and also knowing everyone. Expect a lot of questions from pure strangers. There's little social privacy here."

"I think I learned that yesterday. Friendly bunch."

"They'll gossip you into the ground, but they'll also give up anything to help you." Maggie smiled when he pulled the second plate of food closer and started in on it. "I'll put on coffee right before we open at seven. Have as many refills as you want. It comes with the room."

"Good. I usually like a cup before my run."

An easy silence filled the space between them, until he said, "Look, I'm sorry about last night. I was out of line. If that guy's your boyfriend, just say the word, and I'll back off."

Maggie considered him for a moment. Garth's shoulders

were military straight as his gaze met hers unflinchingly—body language that said he was telling the truth. If she told him Connor was her boyfriend, he'd accept her word and walk out of her life forever without her even telling him about Zach. Panic welled up inside her. That wasn't what she wanted, at least not exactly.

"He isn't my boyfriend," Maggie admitted. "We only recently started dating."

"Good. Because last night . . . I am finding it hard to regret."

His gaze warmed her all over. Did she regret their kiss? It was hard to decide when she was thinking about letting it happen again.

No, she thought. "Garth, I think—"

"No. Don't say anything. I'll be quiet now." His grin had become unrepentant, as if he could read her face. Maybe he could. She'd believed so once.

She concentrated on her breakfast, and they finished at nearly the same time. When she reached for his plates, he gathered them up himself. "I can wash up."

"I have a dishwasher. They just need to be rinsed off and put inside." They did it together, bumping shoulders accidentally. Maggie flushed. How was she ever going to tell him about Zach? She should blurt it out and let him drive away.

Somehow, she couldn't.

"I'm going to make a few calls," Garth said, "but I heard you lost an employee. If you need help here, I don't have any other plans. Just a little exploration."

Maggie laughed. "You learn how to cook in the Air Force?"

"Not anything you'd want to serve here, but I've learned a thing or two bacheloring it these past few years. I make a mean omelet."

"I'll be okay." The last thing she needed was to have him towering over her all day, especially with that kiss scorching her memory.

Nodding, he headed toward the door, where he paused. "If you have time this afternoon or this evening, I'd love to see that lake you talked about."

The air in the kitchen seemed to drain away, because suddenly she found it difficult to breathe. She couldn't go with him so soon. She needed more time to think, to plan. "I may not be able to get away during the day until I replace Hannah."

"Maybe tonight then?"

"Okay." But that seemed wrong. She really needed to check her calendar because she was drawing a complete blank about tonight. All she could think of was how Garth's eyes held hers. *Silly,* she thought.

"Here's my number in case you need it. I can't remember if I put it on the registration paper you had me fill out yesterday." He reached into the single pocket over the left breast of his tee and pulled out a folded sheet of paper she recognized as coming from the small pad she kept in each room. His hands brushed hers as she took it, sending a delicious tingle up her arm.

She put the paper in her apron pocket without looking at it and nodded, not trusting her voice, and turned back to the refrigerator to begin preparing the morning's hash browns. As soon as he was gone, however, she sat down at the table instead. This was going to be a very long day.

She was still sitting and staring at nothing when Charlotte came down, looking bleary-eyed from her night on Maggie's couch bed. "Ugh, how do you get up so early every day?"

"You could have slept in." Maggie bounced to her feet. "What do you want to eat?"

"I couldn't sleep in today; I have to check on Maria's baby. All I want right now is coffee."

"I thought you said you were giving it up? Didn't you say as a midwife you needed to follow your own herbal tea recommendation?"

Charlotte groaned and sank into the chair Garth had vacated. "Some friend you are, throwing my own words at me. That was before I stayed up all night on a sugar high. Remind me never to eat so much ice cream after ten."

"Sorry. I never have problems sleeping."

"That's because you work too hard."

"I keep busy, is all. So you're going out to Maria's right now?"

"Not until eight, but I still have to go home to change and drive out to the Ramos place. And before I do that, I need to wake up."

"I'll get you some." It was a little earlier than Maggie normally put on the coffee, but the café would be open in thirty minutes, and she'd be so busy she might forget anyway.

Minutes later, Charlotte raised her head from the table and gratefully accepted a steaming mug. "Thank you."

As Charlotte drank, Maggie went about the rest of her morning routine. Most everything was prepared during the slow times the day before, but she washed a few more grape clusters for those who preferred that to a mixed fruit bowl. Her bread was nearly ready to go into the ovens.

"You know, I've been thinking," Charlotte said. "If I'd gone to nursing school ten years ago, I'd have a lot more choices and ways to help my ladies without having to run to Doc all the time. Or taking them to the hospital in Panna Creek."

"I thought you've been working with Doc a lot anyway."

"Oh, I have, and he's great, but I can't help thinking a degree would give me more experience and validation."

"I don't know," Maggie said, turning to face her. "Women choose you to deliver their babies because of who you are and the choices you offer."

"Yeah, but once I decide they need more, I'm relegated to being a bystander. If I were a nurse-midwife, it might be a different story. More and more women are choosing the hospital in Panna Creek, even over Doc's clinic or staying home. If I could deliver in the hospital, I wouldn't have to pass them off to someone else."

"Yeah, but some can't make it that far. Or they don't want to leave home. They need someone who can deliver here."

"True." Charlotte came to her feet. "Well, I'd better get home." She waved her fingers at Maggie.

"Thanks for last night."

"If you need me, I'm only a call away."

"I know." Maggie did feel stronger for the support. Charlotte was the best friend she'd ever had, and knowing her was one of the greatest things about living in Forgotten. Before that, it had only been Delitra. *And that's okay,* Maggie thought. She loved where she was right now, and everything she'd gone through had made her the woman she was today. Yes, she would undo some things in her past if she could, but since that was impossible, maybe taking this chance to clear the air with Garth would wash the regret from her soul.

She put the bread in, and by the time she unlocked the café doors at seven, the delicious aroma of baking bread filled the air. Ronica and Fletcher Wilson were her first customers, which meant Fletcher was having another good day.

"Good morning," Maggie sang. "The usual?"

"You look happy this morning," Ronica said as she led Fletcher to a counter stool. "Does that have anything to do with the handsome pilot I saw you with yesterday?"

Maggie gave her a smile. "It's just a beautiful morning, is all."

"That means bug off," Fletcher said with a gentle chuckle. With his elegant facial features, stark white hair, and paper-thin skin, he'd aged well. He looked more like a retired professor than a man who'd farmed the land all his life. Only his brain was giving out.

"Oh, you." Ronica leaned over to kiss his cheek.

Seeing them together, in such stark contrast—Ronica looked more like his daughter now—Maggie remembered a time when it hadn't been that way.

To Maggie, Ronica added, "The usual is fine, only no bread for me today."

"Coming right up."

"I've got some cream and milk in the truck for you. I hope you can use it. I haven't had time to do my normal baking with all the Harvest Festival planning. Will Fletcher be okay here while I go get it?"

"Seriously, woman?" Fletcher said. "You'd think I was a baby, not a farmer. Who do you think milked that cow?"

Ronica looked heavenward. "Not you. You haven't milked a cow in more than five years."

Fletcher shrugged, seemingly unconcerned, and took out the paper he carried under his arm, flipping it open.

"He'll be fine here," Maggie told Ronica. "Come to the kitchen doors, though. That'll save you some steps."

Garth was beginning to worry. Ivy still had not heard from Cora, and a search of nearby streets had yielded no clues to her whereabouts. There had also been no leads from the police.

"They're checking bus stations and the airlines now," Ivy said.

"Kids can't travel alone, can they?"

"For busses, yes. Seventeen and above are counted as adults in most places. And if she bought online, she wouldn't even have to show ID. If she used her name, they'll have a record of it. For airlines, she could have also bought the tickets online. Depending on the airline, they might let her on by herself, but she'd have to show ID, and there would be a paper trail. Her computer's missing, so I can't check to see if she bought anything online—I do have the password. No charges came through on her credit card or any of mine or on Robert's, though. We checked. But even a friend could have bought it for her."

"You want me to come help look for her?"

He counted a silence of a full thirty seconds, a habit developed when dropping bombs in the Air Force. He'd grown quite accurate over the years.

"No," she said finally. "Robert is coming, and you don't know the area. Just let me know if she calls you."

"Okay. But I could call a few guys I know at the base. They can put out an internal alert, at least."

"That would be good. Thank you." Another brief silence, and then she said, "I appreciate you caring. I know this hasn't been easy on you, taking a backseat in Cora's life, and for what it's worth, I'm sorry about that now."

He forced down the anger and frustration that welled up inside him at the comment because reminding her the divorce had been her choice and not his was moot at the moment. "Well, maybe we can talk about making Cora happy once we find her." *If we find her.* Neither said it, but it hung between them nevertheless.

"Yeah. Thanks."

Garth hung up. After years of hoping he could spend more time with Cora, this was not the way he'd envisioned it. He'd thought maybe after high school when she was in college, they'd spend weekends together, or maybe she'd even want to take flying lessons with him. Now he might never have that chance. Maybe he should be glad he and Ivy hadn't conceived again. She'd blamed him, of course. It might even be why she'd left him.

He changed into running pants and went down the back stairs, discarding the idea of his usual morning coffee. Maggie had seemed to have enough on her plate. Outside, the early morning beckoned him with the promise of a beautiful day that wouldn't be too hot or too cold. As he reached the parking lot, he saw the woman from the park yesterday—*Ronica*, he thought—lugging a large crate from a silver truck. He hurried over to help.

"It's mostly the weight of the crate," she said, relinquishing her hold. "Usually my son drops it off when he takes milk to his siblings, but he's not going to be around until later. Plus, there's extra because I haven't had time to make anything with it. Better for Maggie to use it up than to dump it out."

"It comes from your cows?" he asked.

"Just one. My Moona Lisa." She laughed. "You might say she's my baby. My four human babies are all grown up, and she's the only one left. Well, I guess my husband kind of counts as a baby now. Funny how that works." She didn't sound sorry for herself, which made Garth admire her more.

"I believe I had some of that milk this morning. It tasted great."

"Thanks."

Ronica headed toward a door that was ajar behind the outside tables. She opened it wider for him, and he went inside. Maggie was frying up a huge pan of bacon and another of hash browns. In her bright yellow apron, white blouse, and snug jeans, she looked like a ray of sunshine, and his gloom lifted. She was so beautiful, and despite his worry about Cora, he was glad Ivy hadn't wanted him to go to Missouri.

She glanced over at them, doing a slight double-take. "Oh, thanks."

"He saved my bacon," Ronica said. "It's heavier than I thought. Now I'd better get out there and check on Fletcher." She took a few steps past Maggie and craned her neck. "Oh, no. I think he's dumping out one of your saltshakers."

Maggie laughed. "It'll clean." They watched her go.

"Is it always so exciting around here?" he asked.

"Usually it's as boring as watching mud dry." Maggie gave her eyes a slight roll. "But we like it anyway."

He gave a slight chuckle. Boring sounded good to him about now.

Maggie's gaze dropped to his shorts, lingering on his legs. "Running, huh? You want your coffee now?"

"Actually, I'm wound up enough already. I'll get some later." He needed to run, to work out his frustration. It was a coping method that had served him well in the Air Force when he couldn't be up flying.

"Any word on your daughter?"

His daughter. He bit back a bitter retort because it wasn't Maggie's fault he'd been shut out of Cora's life. "No word," he said. "But she'll call me when she can. We have a good relationship." Except when she was hanging up on him like yesterday, but that didn't happen often.

Maggie frowned. "You don't think she was . . . taken?"

"Her stuff's gone. She left on purpose. From there, I don't know."

"I'm really sorry."

He could tell that she was. "Thank you."

He went out the same way he came in and began running at a slow gait. He'd warm up a bit before stopping to stretch. Maybe he should try to find the lake Maggie had talked about. He'd at least head in that direction.

People turned to stare at him as he ran by, as if surprised to see someone running along the sidewalk. Even this early in the morning, people were out and about. He supposed some of them had been up for hours and were coming in to buy feed or eat at the Butter Cake. Unlike on Main Street, this sidewalk was made of cement, but even that soon gave way to dirt, which was easier on his knee that still gave him twinges two years after his last combat mission. He'd bombed an enemy stronghold, survived a crash landing, taken the supplies where they needed to go, stolen an enemy plane, and somehow managed to get all his team home that time, but it hadn't been easy. It was after he'd landed that he'd realized he was weary. Sure, he could carry out missions for five or ten more years, but he felt finished somehow, as if another life awaited. He hadn't known what that was until he'd seen Maggie singing the words he'd once said to her. Now he had to wait to see where this moment took him.

He ran slowly for a mile before doing some stretches and going on at a faster rate, pushing himself to his limit. Already he felt more centered. After another two miles, he hadn't reached a lake, so he stopped to gulp down a bottle of water and check his phone. One text message awaited. He wiped the sweat from his eyes and peered at the screen under the full sun.

I'm safe. I promise. I'm not stupid. Please tell Mom I'm okay, but I'm not going back there. EVER. I'll call you soon. And because I know you'll ask, yes, I had some yummy tacos for breakfast.

Yummy tacos. It was the code he'd worked out with Cora when she was only five, the phrase that either told him she was safe or let her know he'd asked a certain person to pick her up from school. Even so, he called her, but again the line went immediately to voicemail.

"Cora, thank you for texting," he said. "I'm glad you ate tacos. But please call me. We can work this out. Your mom knows how much this means to you now. Look, don't talk to strangers or go anywhere with them. Please. Be safe." His voice cracked a bit at the end.

Sighing, he forwarded Cora's message to Ivy. Then he checked to make sure his phone volume was all the way up before starting back to the café. He was half a block away, running at full speed, when the phone went off, startling him with its loudness.

He slowed to a brisk walk, pulling out the phone and answering it without looking at the number. "Hello?"

"What else did she say?" Ivy demanded.

Disappointment sliced through him. He'd hoped it might be Cora. "Exactly what I sent you," he said. "Nothing more, nothing less."

"Why are you breathing so hard? Are you on the treadmill?"

"I'm outside on a run."

"Oh." She paused a moment before adding, "I guess that's one way to work off the stress. I always wished I could do that."

At least she knew that for him running was like ranting for other people. "Try not to worry too much. As I told you before, she's a smart girl. Even when she's doing something stupid."

Ivy gave a strangled laugh. "That's a weird way of putting it, but yeah, and I think she has you to thank for that. Who knew she'd even remember those silly code words you gave her? We never,

ever sent anyone to pick her up at school without telling her."

"Well, it worked, didn't it?"

"Yes, but now that I know she's safe, I'm mad all over again. But I also know it's partly my fault. I really thought she'd do better here—and she would have if it hadn't been for the incident at school."

"Incident?" He'd arrived at the café and headed toward the outside staircase.

"Oh, no. I'm not telling you about it. She'd kill me. She wasn't happy at school anyway to begin with, but I think what happened was the straw that broke the camel's back."

Garth didn't press because he wouldn't betray Cora's confidence in her place either. "What about news on your side?"

"Well, they found no matching name at the airlines or the bus station. No video footage so far of Cora at the bus stations either. They are interviewing her friends now." She hesitated before adding, "She has a new friend she made working at Subway, and I felt there was some hesitation when I talked to her. I asked the police to start there. I know the other girls well enough to tell if they're hiding anything. Maybe. I feel like I don't know anything anymore."

"I'm sorry you're going through this," he said.

"Thank you."

A silence filled the space between them, but Garth had nothing more to say to her. "Well, let me know if you hear anything, and I'll do the same."

She agreed, and they hung up. For a moment, Garth allowed a sweet nostalgia to run through him. It had been far too long since they'd been a united front.

A cool breeze was drying the sweat on his skin, making it feel tight. What he needed now was a good shower. He jogged up the stairs but had barely gone through the door when he heard screaming downstairs in the café.

Hurrying to the inner staircase, he vaulted down to the main floor, ready to come to Maggie's rescue.

CHAPTER 10

With the construction going on in town, handling breakfast alone was a little more challenging than in the old days, but Ronica stepped up to help with the coffee refills, which made Maggie's job a little easier. After eight, it slowed down as many workers hurried to their jobs, leaving only a few tables of locals and the occasional small group of incoming customers. Easy enough.

Until Fletcher Wilson threw his plate on the floor.

Maggie's plates were made of solid plastic that looked almost like ceramic, and they didn't usually break when accidentally dropped. This one, being hurled, did break—and it sent a piece flying to a table, where it knocked over a glass of orange juice. The woman at the table screamed.

"Fletcher Wilson," Ronica said, raising her voice and hurrying around the counter. "What on earth are you doing?"

"I said I want cinnamon toast!" Fletcher jumped off his stool and nearly fell over, his hands clenched at his sides. He was no longer the refined invalid but a petulant boy with the strength of a man. Maggie had never seen this side of Fletcher, though the rumor mill had been buzzing with hints of it.

"Then you ask me," Ronica reasoned. "You don't throw things. How's Maggie supposed to feed people if you're breaking plates?"

"I already asked," he said.

"No, that was yesterday."

"Well, I want some! And a new newspaper. This one isn't even in English. I can't understand it." Fletcher reached for the steaming glass pot of coffee Ronica had left on the counter, his lip curling.

Maggie hurried toward him, holding her breath, hoping to reach the coffee pot before it ended up on the floor, like her plate. Or worse, in someone's face. Fletcher pulled his arm back to hurl the pot, but as it started forward, two strong hands appeared around his side, one fist closing over his wrist while the other grabbed the pot of coffee. Maggie sighed with relief to see Garth, his hair slicked upward with sweat in a way that shouldn't be sexy but definitely was. His shirt was completely damp.

"Don't move," he said in Fletcher's ear. The old man tried to jerk away, but Garth stepped close, steadying him with his body and holding Fletcher's wrist in place.

"I'll take that," Maggie said, reaching for the coffee. "Fletcher, why don't you come into the kitchen, and I'll get you your cinnamon toast, just like your mama used to make. The bread is fresh out of the oven. Come on. Let's go. Hurry now."

Frowning, the old man released his hold on the coffee pot, and everyone in the café seemed to breathe a sigh of relief. Maggie led Fletcher to the kitchen as Ronica finished picking up the broken plate. "Nothing to see here," Ronica said loudly to the diners. "Go ahead and eat. No, I'll get you a new glass of juice and mop up the table. Sorry about that."

"Look, you sit here," Maggie said to Fletcher in the kitchen, indicating the chair Garth had used that morning, the one closer to the garage door.

"This guy stinks," Fletcher complained. "Keep him away from me."

Garth shrugged. "He's not wrong. I just ran six miles."

"You should probably hit the shower." Maggie couldn't smell anything from where she was cutting the bread.

"I'm not leaving you alone with him."

"Oh, Fletcher's harmless." Or was usually. There had been an incident with a knife a few months back where he'd hurt himself, but that had been an accident. Still, she was suddenly glad Garth remained with her. Fletcher was lean and strong from a lifetime of farm work, even if he had been sick the past couple of years.

Maggie spread butter on a thick slice of bread and set it on her griddle, toasting it before sprinkling on a healthy layer of cinnamon and sugar. "Here you go," she said, keeping her voice bright and even as she set the plate in front of Fletcher. Fletcher grabbed the bread and started munching, making a contented noise in the back of his throat. Maggie decided to make another toast for him.

A few minutes later, Ronica came rushing in, a rag in hand. "I am so sorry! I can't believe he did this."

"Don't worry about it. It's not your fault. Or his." Maggie put her arms around Ronica. "But does he get this way often?"

"Lately, yeah, but at home, everything important or dangerous is put away. He can't help himself. It's just . . ." Ronica blinked back tears. "Oh, I should take him home before anything else happens."

Fletcher stopped eating. "Ronica?" he asked, sounding worried. "What happened? Are you okay?" He looked blankly from her to the others. "Did I do something?"

"No, sweetie." Ronica bent swiftly to kiss his cheek, her short, brown hair swinging over to brush his cinnamon-covered mouth. "Of course not." Straightening, she set her shoulders. "Let's get you home. You can take your bread with you."

"Okay." Fletcher came awkwardly to his feet.

"Can we use the kitchen door?" Ronica asked Maggie. "I don't want to face everyone out there right now."

"Of course." Maggie peeked into the dining room to see if she had new customers, but no one waited at the counter. "I'll put this second toast on a paper plate and carry it out for you."

"Thanks so much." Ronica's smile was forced, and Maggie couldn't blame her. Dementia wasn't an easy road for anyone, but for the survivors, it had to be worse.

Ronica took Fletcher's arm, giving him a little tug in the right direction. He started forward, nodding regally at Maggie as he passed. Such a difference compared to his tantrum in the dining room.

Maggie went with them to the parking lot, and Garth came with her warily, as if expecting something more to happen. She wanted to reassure him, but doing so would only embarrass Ronica more—and Fletcher if he remained lucid.

Fletcher was already in the car and Maggie turning back to the café when a black sedan screeched into the parking lot and came to an abrupt stop behind Ronica's silver truck.

"Isn't that your mayor?" Garth whispered as Josiah Campbell's tall figure unfolded from his car. Maggie nodded.

Josiah hurried toward them. "Is everything okay?" he asked, his dark face drawn. "Someone reported an incident."

Ronica rolled her eyes. "There's no incident. It was just Fletcher wanting toast and thinking he'd already asked for it. He broke a plate and knocked over some juice."

"You're okay, though?" Josiah touched her elbow tentatively.

Ronica's smile held none of the stress she'd displayed moments earlier. "Yes. Thank you. I'm fine. But who told you? It literally just happened."

"Penny Jenkins' daughter Ayleen was eating here, and she texted Penny that Fletcher had an incident. When Penny told me, I came over to see if I could help."

"Penny should remember she's a secretary, not a spy," Ronica shot back.

Josiah chuckled. "You're just mad that she beat you to telling people about it."

"Well, maybe." Ronica was still smiling.

"We ought to look into getting someone to help you with him," Josiah said. "Especially while you've got your hands busy planning city events."

"Don't you dare think about using my Harvest Festival budget for that." Ronica laid her hand on the long sleeve of his arm. "You're a good friend, Josiah, but I can take care of Fletcher."

Josiah stared at his arm as if mesmerized by her touch. Maggie turned away in embarrassment, but Ronica was already opening the door to her truck. She waved as she drove off.

"Would you like some breakfast, Josiah?" Maggie offered.

His face relaxed. "You know what? I think I will. But I'll send someone to get it. I've got a meeting in a few minutes." With a nod, he hurried back to his car.

Maggie turned and nearly ran into Garth. "What's up with those two?" he asked. "I could feel the sparks from clear over here."

So could Maggie, but she wasn't sure Ronica or Josiah were aware of it themselves. No one gave Josiah's marriage much chance of surviving, but for the time being, he was still married and faithful. In turn, Ronica was devoted to her husband, regardless of his mental aptitude. Life might not be fair, but they were honorable people.

"Nothing," Maggie said. "They're good friends."

"Okay. If you say so."

She caught a whiff of Garth's odor as they neared the kitchen. Instead of repelling her, it reminded her of their long day together, when they'd danced and wandered through Trenton's waterfront streets until all hours. Her stomach ached with a strange sort of longing, but she said, "I think Fletcher was right about you needing that shower."

Garth chuckled. "Okay, I get the hint. See you later." He angled toward the back stairs while she went into the kitchen.

Inside the café, Maggie had customers waiting, chatting amiably at the cash register—two old-timers, Larry and Sam, who'd retired from ranching some years back and often found their way to the Butter Cake to dawdle over a cup of coffee.

They turned as one when they saw her. "We were over at Town Hall and heard you had some excitement," Larry said. "Looks like we missed everything, though."

"You did at that. What can I get you?"

"Aren't you even going to tell us what happened?" Sam asked. Unlike Larry, whose receding hairline had met his bald spot, he still had a full head of gray hair.

Larry snorted. "You know it's no use asking her." He nudged his buddy. "Come on. We'll find out the story from them over there." He pointed to one of the two tables that still had customers.

"We just want coffee," Sam said to Maggie.

"Today I want bread too," Larry countered. "A thick piece with lots of butter. Your bread smells like a slice of heaven and tastes even better."

Sam nodded. "Oh, yeah. Sound's good. Me too. Heat them a bit so the butter melts. You know how we like it."

Maggie put two cups, a tiny pitcher of fresh cream, and the coffee pot on a tray. "Come on, you two. Let's get you seated." She led them to their usual spot near the windows, right next to one of the occupied tables. After pouring Sam's coffee black and topping Larry's off with a healthy dose of cream, she paused at the other table. "Can I get you anything else?" They declined, so she took their credit card and rang up their bill.

She barely had Larry and Sam's bread on their table before a new group of three women entered, which sent her back to the kitchen to cook more bacon, eggs, and hash browns. She hadn't yet finished the order when another group came in, staring interestedly around the café. Probably wanting the scoop on Fletcher.

"Be right with you," she sang out.

Before she could take their order, another group of five men from the construction site entered, looking hungry. Telling herself that she'd better hire someone to replace Hannah sooner rather than later, Maggie laid out a pound of bacon in her pan and was cracking eggs when a figure behind her made her jump.

"Sorry." Garth gave her an unrepentant smile. "I should have called out a warning or something." He spread out his hands. "How do I look?"

Maggie stifled a laugh. He was wearing one of her butter-colored aprons over his white button-up shirt and jeans, but he was considerably taller than the women who worked here, so it was rather small on his chest. With his wide shoulders and military stance, he definitely looked out of place.

He held up his hand to stop her reply. "Never mind. I know I look ridiculous, but at least I got the dress code right. Except I don't own any boots—not of the cowboy variety anyway."

Maggie lifted one of her sandaled feet. "We don't wear those in the Butter Cake. But why are you wearing my apron?"

"I noticed you're short a hand this morning, and I told you I cook a mean omelet."

"What about regular eggs? Can you scramble them?"

"Like the ones you did this morning?"

She nodded. "I need a dozen."

"Yep."

She left him to it as she turned the hash browns and poured the drinks. When she filled the plates, his egg pieces were slightly larger than hers, but they were perfectly cooked instead of being overdone.

"Nice," she said.

With a little encouragement, she convinced the next customers to try his omelets. "Always willing to help vet a new chef," they joked.

Garth took up the challenge with flare, liberally using her diced onions, cubed cheese, and leftover ham from dinner. When she went to heat up bread to go along with the omelet, she ran right into him, and his hands went out to steady her.

"Sorry," she said.

"No problem." He gave her a little bow. He'd also done that at the riverfront dance, when they twirled around like idiots, laughing and tripping over each other. She half expected him to step close now and twirl her around like he had then and fought a stab of disappointment when he didn't. The thoughts made her flush under his intense stare. What was wrong with her?

Despite the unwelcome flashbacks, they fell into a surprisingly easy routine as Garth quickly picked up the food preparation. Not that there was a lot to learn. In terms of breakfast, she didn't offer a huge variety. Of course, she was always willing to do something special for her customers—like use butter instead of bacon grease to cook the scrambled eggs or pour Larry and Sam their fourth cups of coffee.

"Aren't you afraid you'll die of caffeine overdose?" she asked them.

"Naw," Sam said. "We're afraid if we don't drink it, we won't be able to get out of bed."

"Everyone dies," Larry added. "Better to go quick than to lose your marbles like old Fletcher."

"It's a darn shame." Sam blew on his coffee. "He's fifteen years younger than I am. If he clings on that long, it's going to be a lot of years for his poor wife. Especially if this mean streak of his gets worse."

Sam nodded. "I hear it sometimes does."

"Well, Ronica's a good woman," Maggie said. "If anyone can take care of Fletcher, it's her. If you need any more coffee, let me know."

At ten-forty, Keisha hurried into the café and dove in the back for an apron. "Sorry I'm late. I was taking a quiz." She blinked at Garth. "Hello. Are you our newest employee?"

"No, he's just helping out. I don't know what I'd have done without him. We'd better get some bites on your ad soon." Maggie threw a wet rag at her. "The tables need to be cleaned."

Keisha looked Garth up and down. "Seriously? You should use him out front. He'd get a lot of tips."

Garth snorted. "Uh, I don't think so."

"You sure?" Keisha smiled flirtatiously.

"Let me rephrase," Garth said. "Never, no way, no dice." They all laughed.

By the time Keisha cleaned up the tables, the customers had thinned, and there was no need for Maggie to leave the kitchen. She busied herself tossing the ingredients for her spinach soup into a large pan. She'd prepped the vegetables yesterday, and usually the soup would have been simmering by now, but without Hannah here she hadn't been able to start it. Yesterday's soup would have to be enough until the new one was done. She put a pan on the stove and began reheating the leftovers.

Now that the rush had died, her big kitchen suddenly felt too small with Garth looming over her, and she found herself stepping into his path far too often. It didn't help that the vision of dancing with him hovered in her mind like some kind of ghostly haunting.

"I think I'm in the way now," he said after finishing his last omelet. He untied his apron and handed it to her.

"I appreciate your help." She threw the apron into the basket of dirty ones she washed every couple of days.

"You're welcome." He looked at his phone and frowned.

Maggie felt suddenly chastened. Here she'd been thinking only of the café while he was still worried about his daughter. "Have you heard anything from Cora?"

"Actually, yes. With all that happened, I forgot to tell you. She texted me during my run and said she's okay, but she won't pick up when I call. I think her phone is off."

"But how do you . . . you're sure it's her?"

"Yeah. We have a code word."

"That's smart."

He shrugged. "Military work tends to spread to your private life. We used them on missions."

"I can imagine that." But she could only imagine because her own military father hadn't bothered to show back up in her life after deserting her mother when she was a toddler. All Maggie had was imagination. She hadn't even known he was dead until she'd applied for US Citizenship before Zach's birth. She'd missed meeting him by a year.

"When Cora was small, it was more a game we played than anything else," Garth said. "Never really needed it. Well, until now." He plunged his hands into his pockets and rocked back on his heels.

"I bet she loved it."

"Not according to her." His chuckle warmed her. "But I'm glad now."

Keisha laid an order form in the small window opening between the kitchen and counter areas. Maggie glanced at the order—a sandwich and a bowl of soup. As she began building the perfect sandwich, she looked up to see Garth staring hungrily at it.

"Why don't you go sit out at the counter? I'll make you an early lunch. On the house." She ladled a bowl of soup, put it on a tray with the sandwich, and passed it to Keisha, who appeared in the doorway to grab it. Not for the first time Maggie fleetingly thought about making the order window larger to accommodate the trays.

"I am kind of hungry," he admitted.

"Any kind of meat in particular?"

He shook his head. "Nah. Surprise me."

She turned toward the bread, but his hand reached out to take hers. Gently, not forcibly. "That day in Trenton, you didn't give me your contact information. Was that because of your father?"

She knew the answer without thinking about it. "Yes. Mostly." Their time had been amazing, but she'd made up her mind years earlier not to wait around for any man. She'd waited long enough. "But also because I was young. I didn't know . . ."

His thumb rubbed over the top of her hand, achingly light. Her entire body seemed to vibrate in answer. "Didn't know what?" he pressed. "Didn't know you'd regret meeting me so much? Regret what we did?"

Keisha took that moment to slap another form down in the order window.

Maggie didn't look away from Garth. "I didn't regret meeting you."

"Then what?"

I didn't know I'd never find that feeling again. But not in a million years would she admit that to him. "I'd better get this order."

He let her go then, and Maggie hurried to grab Keisha's order, reading it quickly. A late breakfast, which meant more eggs she could make on autopilot. Good.

"Go on and get whatever you want to drink from Keisha," she told Garth. "I'll be right out with your sandwich."

"Thanks."

She turned back toward the stove, but not before she heard the softest of sighs escape his lips. She had to tell him the rest. The truth. They both deserved closure. *I'll do it tonight,* she thought. Even if it meant he'd flee the café to get away from her in the morning.

She cooked the bacon breakfast while putting together Garth's turkey and roast beef sandwich. Strange how he was basically a complete stranger, yet she knew he didn't like ham on his sandwiches or pickles and mayo. They'd had club sandwiches that

day in Trenton, and teasing him about the way he'd drowned
the bread in mustard and how much he hated the large pickles
served on the side had been deliciously fun. Who on earth didn't
like pickles? Well, he'd certainly kissed her after she'd eaten hers.
In fact, he hadn't even waited for her to finish, seeming to need
to taste her between each bite.

Smiling, she finished the sandwich, dished up the breakfast
plate, and dumped fresh fries and a mound of salad next to Garth's
sandwich. Balancing both meals, she went out to the front, where
Keisha was talking to Garth, who was holding a soft drink.

"Thank you!" Keisha grabbed the breakfast plate. While she
took it out to her customer, Maggie slid the sandwich in front
of Garth.

"Ranch dressing?" she asked. At his nod, she grabbed the
dressing from the counter refrigerator, where they also kept the
juices, placing the bottle in front of him so he could squeeze on
as much as he liked.

"This is some sandwich," Garth said.

"The bigger the better, I say."

He peered closer. "Tomatoes, roast beef, turkey, mustard,
lettuce, olives, two kinds of cheese—hey, what about pickles?"

"You hate pickles."

His grin was teasing. "Ah, so you remember the pickles. Well,
guess what? I love pickles now. I learned to like them after . . .
you know. No. I learned to love them." He winked. "I was going
to be ready the next time we met."

The next time, which had been too late. Her smile wavered.

"I'd like triple pickles now, thank you very much," he said.

That brought her smile back. "Seriously?"

"I'm very serious about my pickles. Don't blame me. It's your
fault. You got me hooked."

"Coming right up." Back inside her kitchen, she filled a small plate with pickle slices cut the long way.

"That's more like it," Garth said with an appreciative wink. "I need more mustard, though. You hardly put any on. And I like it with my fries."

"You're crazy. There's already twice what anyone else would put on." She turned back to the counter refrigerator to grab the mustard, setting it on the counter with a loud *plop!*

"Double isn't nearly enough." He picked up one of the pickles and took a bite. She couldn't take her eyes from his lips. "Want some?" he offered, his expression taunting.

She was saved from answering when Keisha returned from wiping a table. "We don't have much time before the lunch rush, but did you get a chance to make the filling for those eclairs? The ladies will have the shells done by five."

Maggie stared, her stomach sinking. "Oh, no. I forgot. I was going to make it this morning after the bread, wasn't I?"

"That's okay," Keisha said. "Hannah's still coming after school today to help out for the party, and we can put together the cold cut platters while you make the custard. You can fill them after we close while we set up."

"Does this mean no lake tonight?" Garth asked.

"I'm afraid so," Maggie said. "I forgot we're closing an hour early tonight because our Chief of Police asked us to host his wife's surprise birthday party. We're in charge of all the refreshments. But don't worry, you're invited. We're all allowed to bring a plus one."

"Are you asking me out?" he teased.

Keisha laughed. "You can be my plus one instead. I'm not seeing anyone, and you'd actually be doing me a favor. Chief

McColl keeps trying to set me up with Ronica's son, and we have nothing in common. Can you see me as a farmer's wife?"

Garth chuckled. "Well, I'm pleased to accept both your offers, if you don't mind sharing me."

"Whatever." Maggie rolled her eyes.

Garth picked up another pickle and offered it to her as a group of customers entered the café doors. "I saved this one for you."

Taking the challenge, Maggie leaned forward and took a bite before heading back into the kitchen, leaving him staring after her.

At least their discussion would be put off until after the party.

CHAPTER 11

G arth checked his phone for what seemed like the hundredth time that day. Nothing was more frustrating than waiting for a rebellious teen to check in—unless it was spending the morning working with a woman you were crazy attracted to and who didn't seem to share the feeling. But he hadn't imagined her response last night. Or had he?

After lunch, he'd busied himself walking around the town, chatting with strangers, and calling Ivy for information. The bright spot in all that was a tip from Cora's new friend at Subway that Cora might have gotten a ride from Arnold to St. Louis with the friend's cousin, which meant maybe she was staying with one of her old friends there. She might even be heading to her father's house, though he had denied seeing her.

Cora, please, he had texted after hearing about St. Louis.

No reply.

Maybe she was worried about the police tracking her phone. It could happen, especially if the colonel he'd called this morning pulled in any favors.

He glared at the screen. Still nothing.

Nothing except a text from his mom about when he'd be back in Florida and if he was planning to spend Thanksgiving with them. He'd already told her he had no idea what job he'd have by then, but if at all possible he would be there. He'd missed too many holidays with family. Even when he'd been in the States, with the tension between him and his father, they'd usually gone to Ivy's family instead. He'd changed that in the past six years, and he knew how much it meant to his mother. Losing access to Cora, her only granddaughter, had been tough on her, and he would do anything now to alleviate that.

He spent the rest of the afternoon driving around Forgotten and familiarizing himself with the area. The new pasta factory west of Main Street teemed with construction workers, a line of pre-fabricated trailers signaling where they slept. The nearby housing settlement under construction wasn't nearly as busy, but the half-finished houses looked modern compared to the rest of the town. He supposed it was a good thing, but so far the houses looked like little clones of each other. Next, he drove east, past the Butter Cake, following the signs to Forgotten Reservoir, hoping to find a better place for tomorrow's run. The fields he passed were lush and green, perhaps ready to harvest.

The road to the reservoir forked, and he chose left toward Chelsea Park. There he found bushes of all sizes, wildflowers with lush stems, and verdant grass. Beyond a short, rocky beach, dazzling turquoise water gleamed as it reflected the overhead sun. A literal forest bordered the lake.

There had to be a path here that would make a more enjoyable run, but he was curious where the other fork went. He turned back and followed it, soon reaching houses built along the lake's edge. No cookie-cutter houses here, only beautiful old cottages and cabins, mixed in with newer houses that also included some frontier charm. One property had a for sale sign, and on a whim, he drove down the drive, disappointed to find a ruined cabin with only three sides standing and a single broken window too small for any fire code.

Farther on, he spied a second sale sign, and that property featured a timeless log cabin. The structure looked sound, but the vegetation was slowly encroaching. He took one of the fliers, wondering how good the fishing was. He'd never actually tried fishing except once as a boy in scouts, though he loved eating fish. Maybe it was time to pick up a hobby. Glancing at the price on the flier, he was stunned to see the cabin and the half acre of land was a fourth of the price he'd paid for his Florida condo, which had come with only a postage-sized piece of land.

The reservoir was far larger than he'd expected. If the area ever boomed, this property would skyrocket. Not that he was in the market. Walking down to the lake to a dock made of the same logs as the cabin, he saw a few boats with people fishing. Nothing with an engine, though, and he wondered if they were permitted. He'd seen a boat rental shack in the park, so maybe he'd take one out. Would Maggie go with him?

After a little more sightseeing, he headed back to the café where two teens were managing the front counter—a talkative girl with red hair and numerous freckles and an Asian girl named Lisa that he'd met at dinner the night before. They had his meal out from the kitchen within minutes, which told him Maggie and whoever else was with her were cooking ahead.

The taste of his steak made him want to groan with pleasure.

He'd give Maggie credit—she was really good at this. Did feeding people make her as happy as singing had? He hoped so.

He'd barely finished half his meal when the red-haired teen clapped her hands together and raised her voice. "Okay, everyone, it's six now and we are officially closed. As the sign on the door says, there's a private party here tonight. Thank you for coming. When you're finished, we can ring you up." She hurried to the door and turned over the *OPEN* sign. "If you're invited to the party tonight, you'll need to come back at seven. That's when we'll be opening the doors again."

Her announcement was met with good-natured groans, but people began taking out their wallets from pockets and purses. A few waited for her to come to them; others went to the register themselves. Soon Garth was the last customer in the café that was suddenly quiet, except for some banging of pans and occasional laughter coming from the kitchen. Garth had a glimpse of Maggie as she crossed the doorway.

The red-haired teen plopped herself on a stool on the counter opposite him as Lisa disappeared into the kitchen with the cash register drawer. "You're the pilot, huh? I wasn't working last night, so I didn't get to meet you. I'm Ingrid Patterson." She held out her hand, her pale blue eyes piercing his. Her wide smile made her freckles run together in a way that was endearing.

"That's me," he said. "I'm Garth. Nice to meet you, Ingrid."

"So were you in a war? Do you have any medals?"

"A few."

"A few what? Medals or wars?" She laughed at her own words.

"Both," he said. "I was mostly in Afghanistan, off and on. But other places too."

"And the medals?"

People always wanted to know about those, and maybe they did say something about the soldier, but not always. "Yeah. I've got medals. Maybe I'll show them to you one day. Each has its own story." A few he'd earned through flying a certain number of missions while others were more challenging. He was most proud of the Medal of Honor because he'd saved his crew and the mission despite his severe knee and chest injury. The others weren't as special, like one of his Purple Hearts he'd earned simply by surviving after getting hit by shrapnel. That one he wasn't so proud of.

"Okay," said Ingrid. "I'll hold you to it."

He felt stupid even as she spoke. He had no business referring to the future when he didn't even know how long he'd be in town.

"Come on," Lisa beckoned as she returned with the empty register drawer. "We need to get the decorations up. And pull down the blinds, so the chief's wife won't see everything before she comes in."

Having nothing better to do, Garth helped the girls put up foil banners, streamers, and balloons. Maggie emerged from the kitchen, the elastics holding back her hair dangerously close to falling out.

She nodded a greeting at Garth before saying, "This looks really great, girls. The flowers just arrived. Set one on each table before you go home to change, okay? And if you could hurry back to help us set out the food, that would be great. We also need to change."

"Is this a black-tie event?" Garth quipped.

"Hardly," Ingrid said with a roll of her eyes, "but it is best dress, which means dresses for us."

"Why don't you girls go home and change already," he said.

"I'll put out the flowers." To Maggie, he added, "They'll need more prep time than I will. There's not enough makeup in the world to make my skin smooth."

Ingrid and Lisa laughed and stared at Maggie with pleading eyes. "Okay, go," she said.

The kitchen was an organized mess, with Keisha and Hannah putting together platters that they placed in the fridge or inside a couple of large coolers, and Maggie filling eclairs. By the time he finished with the flowers, Maggie and Hannah had disappeared, and a huge pink birthday cake sat on one of the counters.

"They went upstairs to change," Keisha told him. "I'll do the same as soon as I finish laying out this fruit."

He glanced down at his jeans. "Not sure I brought much in the way of dress clothes."

Her eyes followed his. "The shirt you're wearing is fine. If you have black pants, believe me, that's all you'll need. This is Forgotten, and most men's idea of dressing up is using their good boots and washing behind their ears. A few of the older men will wear their church suits, but it's only the women who really dress up. And the mayor and local attorneys, of course."

Garth laughed. "Good to know."

"Oh, but put this cake on the counter, okay? One of the ladies had her husband drop it off."

After doing as she requested, he went upstairs, glancing at Maggie's closed door before ducking into his own room, where he showered and shaved. Looking over the clothes he'd brought, he grabbed the black slacks he'd worn yesterday and a blue and black pinstriped shirt, which if Keisha had been telling the truth, would be more than dressy enough.

Was the aftershave overkill? Well, too late now.

He checked his phone and found a text had come in from Ivy

while he'd been in the shower. *Cora did get a ride to St. Louis and spent the night at her friend's cousin's place. They claim to have dropped her off at the bus station this morning, and cameras there caught her briefly, but they don't know where she went or if she got on a bus. Do you think she's trying to go to your place in Florida?*

How was he supposed to know that? Wait, he'd told Cora he wasn't home. Would she try to come here? But that would be ridiculous. Forgotten was out in the middle of nowhere, and in fact someone had told him the bus only came once a week on Wednesday morning, which would have been today, and even then it dropped people off sixteen miles out of town. Not exactly accessible for a teenager.

No, he texted Ivy. *She knows I'm not there. She asked to come see me.*

A response came immediately: *Why didn't you tell me that?*

Why would I? It doesn't make a difference.

Where are you?

He was tempted to say, "With the woman I've always loved," but that seemed a bit vindictive. *A small town in Kansas visiting an old friend.*

Where in Kansas? Maybe she went there.

Had he told Cora the name of the town? He couldn't remember. *Forgotten,* he texted.

What do you mean forgotten? You can't forget where you are!

The town is called Forgotten. It's in Kansas, and they only have a bus come here on Wednesday mornings, so she can't be coming here. After no response to this, he added, *Look, I have a thing to attend, but I'll keep my phone handy. Bye.*

Sliding the phone into his pocket, he ran a comb through his hair. He looked like something from an Air Force recruitment video, so he shook his head to loosen his hair a bit. He was ready.

Another text came through as he reached the door.

What thing?

He stared at the text. Ivy had always been blunt, but for years now she hadn't cared where he was or what he was doing. The odd question made him uneasy. He wasn't going down *that* road ever again. Deliberately, he deleted the message without responding.

It was after seven, and people were already gathering in the café dining space, but the lights were dim, and they were talking in hushed voices. About twenty women present were wearing dresses of different kinds, from homemade to designer—at least as far as he could tell. The dozen men were combed and wearing good boots, but a few wore jeans. Nods came in his direction as he recognized some of the people he'd seen around town, including Ronica Wilson, who he'd helped this morning with her husband and the milk, but her husband wasn't with her.

Maggie came from the kitchen with a large platter of cold cuts and cheeses. She looked stunning in a sleeveless black dress that followed the lines of her figure, ending shortly above her knee. Her hair was down around her shoulders, thick and straight and shiny, and her makeup highlighted her dark eyes. She could have been on any stage in the world and looked perfectly at home. The only thing slightly out of place was the glimpse of a gold necklace that disappeared into the high neckline of her dress instead of lying on the outside. Maybe she'd forgotten to pull it out, though now that he thought about it, he seemed to recall glimpsing the same chain on her neck earlier. If so, the pendent it must hold had been hidden then too.

Time slowed as she approached, radiating as if from within, and Garth had to remind himself to breathe.

"Hey," she said to him as he stepped forward on the other side of the counter to help her place the heavy dish between a tray of breads and a platter of fruit. "You look nice." Her smile alone was reward for his effort.

"Well, you're nothing short of stunning," he responded.

Her eyes lowered, refusing to meet his. "Thank you."

Had he offended her? Or made her feel self-conscious? The Maggie he'd known would have uttered a flirtatious comeback. Something like, "Oh yeah? Why don't you come here and show me exactly how stunning?" Or was that the Maggie he'd created in his mind?

Another thought occurred to him. Maybe she felt threatened. Yes, he was impatient to know what she was holding back, but he wasn't the kind of man to force a woman. Not for any reason. Surely she understood that.

"I have a few more things to get ready," Maggie said, lifting her eyes again. "The McColls will be here any moment."

"What time are they coming exactly?" asked Ingrid, the red-haired waitress, appearing next to Garth like magic, as if whatever barrier separating them from the others in the room had dissolved away.

"About twenty after seven, I believe." Maggie reached inside her dress and took out a gold pocket watch supported by the gold chain Garth had glimpsed earlier.

Pocket watch. Garth's breath caught in his throat. *His pocket watch.*

She opened the lid briefly before snapping it shut. "Looks like any minute now. I'd better grab the plates." Maggie had begun to put the watch back inside her dress when her gaze brushed his, stopping, her eyes going wide. At once he understood why. She hadn't meant to look at the watch in front of him. She hadn't wanted him to know she still had it after all these years.

Their gazes held. He watched emotions run over her face: worry, relief, resignation . . . and something more he couldn't identify. With deliberation, she released the watch to let it fall onto her dress to rest between her breasts, looking like it should have been there all along. Then, just as deliberately, she turned and walked back into her kitchen.

She had his watch—his great-grandfather's watch. A rueful smile came unbidden to his lips. He'd given it to Maggie before leaving her that day. He'd wrapped her in his arms and begged her to give him her address and phone number—or did she have an email? Anything. After her utter refusal of his proposal, her contact information was the only chance he had left, but she'd simply laughed and told him it was for her to know and him to find out. Making her take the pocket watch, the only thing of value he owned, had been his desperate way to remain connected with her.

So he'd kissed her and slipped it into her hand, whispering against her cheek. "I'll find you."

It wasn't until years later, back in the States, that he learned the watch was solid gold, instead of a lesser family keepsake entrusted to him. He'd endured a lot of heartache when his father learned he no longer had the watch, but he'd eventually been forgiven because, after all, he'd come home alive when others hadn't. Plus, he'd married Ivy and given his parents Cora, their first and only granddaughter.

Seeing the pocket watch now gave him hope—hope that this something between them wasn't only in his head.

"Here they come!" Maggie announced in a hushed shout. "Quiet, everyone!" Silence fell as people stared at the front door. They could hear steps outside and voices.

"Are you sure Maggie's even here?" a woman said. "It's kind of dark."

"I told her we'd stop by on our way to the restaurant. Look, the door is open." The door swung outward, and a diminutive blond woman came inside the café on tall heels, followed by a big man in a shapeless suit. Someone hit the lights as the room exploded into a chorus of happy birthdays.

"Oh, my!" The woman looked around at the partygoers, her face bursting into a smile. She turned to her husband. "You sneaky little trickster. I should have known something was up." She hugged him. The two looked a little incongruous. She was petite, curvaceous, and pale, and her red dress fit like it was made for her, while he was tall, big, and red-faced, and his suit was far too large. But somehow when he returned her hug, they fit perfectly.

"Happy birthday," he said. That set off another chorus of well wishes.

Garth watched as the couple, never far apart, greeted the guests. Food, drinks, and presents began flowing. Someone started music. Eventually, the guest of honor made her way to Garth, and Maggie appeared out of nowhere with introductions.

"This is my friend, Garth Dalton," she said. "He's staying at the Butter Cake for a few days. Garth, this is Natalie McColl, the birthday girl, and this is her husband and our Chief of Police, Caleb McColl."

"Nice to meet you," Garth said. At least he wasn't only a guest anymore but had been upgraded to friend. "And happy birthday."

"Thank you. It's nice to meet you too." Natalie's smile radiated light.

"How's Joni?" Maggie asked.

Natalie gave a little shrug. "Still not doing too well. Her digestion, you know. She sleeps a lot, and she's lost too much weight.

We're trying different things. I have a lot of hope we'll pin it down soon."

"Hopefully, you can find out what's wrong. But that's too bad. I'd hoped to see her here tonight."

"Me too," Caleb said.

Natalie laughed. "If you do see her, make sure to call her Angelica. She's really adamant about her new name."

"Oh, of course." Maggie laughed with them.

The couple talked a bit more before moving off. "So," Garth said when they were alone, unable to wait a moment longer. "You still have the watch."

"Yes." She nodded, looking out over the crowd and not at him.

"I'm glad you kept it."

Her face turned toward him. "It was a good day."

"It was." He wanted to touch the watch, to hold it in his hand and become reacquainted, but something stronger urged him to let it ride. He didn't want to ruin the ease between them.

"Something to eat?" she asked.

He laughed. "After that dinner you gave me? I couldn't."

"You have to at least have an éclair."

"Maybe I can find room for one of those."

When people had seemed to have their fill of food and drink, they sang *Happy Birthday* and cut the cake before dimming the lights and pushing back the tables for dancing. It wasn't a huge space, but the crowd had only swelled to fifty.

Garth refused cake and turned to Maggie. "Dance?"

She pinned him without expression for too long, and he squirmed under her penetrating gaze. "Okay," she said finally.

A rowdy country song began, but the challenge didn't deter him. He had little experience with country dancing—and most of that had been back in Trenton with Maggie—but he was going to try. She was better than he was, and her swaying hips mesmerized him. Being with her now, dancing this way, was every bit as good as it had been on the day they'd met, as if she belonged next to him. Maybe tonight they would finally talk, and he'd know if a future was possible.

An odd ringing penetrated their dance, and it took him a moment to realize it was coming from his vibrating pocket. He stopped, reaching for it and checking the caller ID. One glimpse of the name, and urgency filled him. "It's Cora. I need to take this."

"Of course." Maggie walked over to the front of the café with him.

"Cora," he said, holding the phone tightly against his ear. "Where are you?"

A voice came to him—a tearful voice, but he couldn't understand anything over the music. "Sweetie, just a minute. I'm going somewhere I can hear you."

Maggie was already holding open the front door, and he darted through with a grateful nod. He barely noticed the door closing behind him. "Okay," he said, trying to be calm. "Are you there? What's going on?"

"I'm here . . . and I'm okay . . . and I don't know why I'm crying . . . It's just, when I heard your voice . . . Daddy, can you come get me?"

"Yes. Yes, of course. Where are you?"

"I'm in Lincoln, Nebraska at the bus station. I just got here. I was trying to get a local bus to where you are, but there isn't one until next week! And it's already dark."

"Listen, honey, is the bus station still open?"

"Yeah. But it's a metal building and parking lot and not much more," Cora said. "I don't know what to do."

"Are you inside?"

"Yeah."

"Then stay right where you are. I'm coming to get you. Do you think you have enough phone battery left to keep talking to me?"

"I had my phone off mostly, so I wouldn't run out—and so Mom wouldn't sick the police on me. But there's an outlet here, so yeah. And don't worry. I have my pepper spray."

He smiled despite his concern. "Okay, then hold on a minute. I need to make sure I'll be able to get into my room here when we get back."

"Are you going to tell Mom?"

"You know I have to."

"But not right this second, right? It's not like she can get to me faster than you."

She had a point. "Let's talk about this in a moment. Hold on."

Garth went back inside to find Maggie talking to Keisha by the door. "I have to drive to Lincoln. I'll be back late. Will I be able to get in?"

"Your key to the outside door at the top of the stairs will work at any hour," Maggie said. "But is everything okay?"

For the first time he realized the knot in his gut was gone. "Yes, I think so. I'm going to get Cora."

CHAPTER 12

C ora repeatedly refused to call her mother on her own, and after fifteen minutes of conversation, Garth gave in to her plea to be the one to make the call.

Ivy answered on the second ring, her voice laden with sleep. "You find her?"

"Yes." It was nearly ten-thirty for both of them, which wasn't late when your teenage daughter was missing, but he suspected Ivy might have been sleeping for the first time since Cora's absence. "She's safe. I'm driving to get her now."

"Where is she?"

"Just over the Kansas border from me in Lincoln, Nebraska. She took the bus there."

"Is she okay?"

"So far. But I'd like to get her back on the phone while I drive. She's at the station alone, and I have no idea if they close soon or what. I might be breaking a few speed limits."

"Why didn't she call me?"

"You know why."

"Because she hates me." Tears peppered her voice.

"She's safe. We can work everything else out."

Silence came over the line, and then, "You need to put her on the next plane and get her back here."

"I could do that. But would it be okay to wait a day? It might give her time to calm down a little. I don't mind watching over her."

"Yeah, or incite her against me." Her bitterness stabbed at him.

He fought down indignance. "That's unfair. I'm calling you, aren't I? You know that's not me."

Another long pause. "Okay. You're right. I'm sorry. Things have just been so crazy."

"There aren't going to be any flights tonight anyway. Besides, the place where I'm staying is a two-hour drive from Lincoln. She'll need sleep. Won't Friday be soon enough?" *Or even Saturday or Sunday,* he thought, which would likely give them a better price on airfare, but now wasn't the time to mention that. Ivy would probably think of it herself after she was sure Cora was safe.

She sighed. "Okay, but text me the minute you lay eyes on her."

"I will. And I'll get her to call you, but it probably won't be tonight. It'll be after midnight before I even get there."

"Okay. At least I'll know she's okay."

It said something that Ivy trusted him with Cora's physical well-being. "I'll text you soon."

He called Cora back, and for the next hour and forty minutes they talked about everything—everything except what had happened at school that had made her run away after only a week.

She came out of the building as he parked, and they ran to each other. Her mascara was smeared and her long brown hair a mess, but she looked okay. He hugged her tightly. Cora had never been a thin child, but she seemed to have lost a little weight in the months since he'd last seen her.

"I'm okay," she murmured as she drew away. "Sorry for making you leave your party."

He took both the backpack and the duffle she carried, slinging them over his shoulder. "Not my party, and I don't mind."

She hugged him again. "That's what I love about you. Mom would be making a list of the ways I'd inconvenienced her, and even if it would be true, it's not exactly encouraging."

He fought a smile. Cora had her mother pegged. "That reminds me, I need to send her a text." He did it one-handed, keeping an arm around Cora.

"I'm not talking to her," she declared. "Not tonight."

"I know." He waited until they got into the Jeep to say, "You didn't think she'd let you come visit me if you asked?"

"Not during school. And this isn't a visit. I want to live with you." Her jaw jutted forward as if daring him to protest.

"Live with me?" he repeated, stunned.

She nodded, her jaw still clenched.

Not knowing what to say to that, he started the engine. He was considering finding a place to crash in town, despite what he'd told Ivy, but maybe they needed the two-hour drive back to Forgotten to discuss the situation. He put the Jeep into gear and navigated to the highway.

"You don't want me, do you?" she whispered into the darkness.

When he glanced over at her, she was no longer defiant but deflated and sad. Her blue eyes looked black in the darkness. "Of course I do. You're always welcome to live with me. I consider myself your father. You know that."

She sighed. "Yeah, I guess."

"But your mother has custody, and your birth father too."

"No, he doesn't. Not anymore. I don't even have to see him if I don't want."

He considered that. "Okay, but until you're eighteen, your mother has the final say. That doesn't mean we can't talk to her about options, though. She loves you."

"It doesn't seem like it."

"Well, she does. And she has always put you first." Garth squinted at the lights of an oncoming car. "But this isn't just about a new school, is it? Are you going to tell me what happened?"

"It *is* about the new school." Her voice cracked. "It's a horrible place, and the people are even more horrid!"

"Okay, I believe you." He glanced at her and then back at the road. "Are you going to tell me what happened? You know I'm on your side."

She waited for several long seconds before nodding. "Well, there's this boy, a really cute boy."

Of course, a boy would be involved—he'd seen that coming a mile away. He waited for more.

"But it's not what you're thinking," Cora continued. "He talked to me once at lunch, is all. Said he was leaving and that I could have his seat. The next thing I know, this really fake girl comes over to me. You know the kind—perfect blond hair, fake nails, and eyelashes out to here." She made a motion, and he glanced over to see her finger a few inches from her eyes. "A cheerleader, of course. She asked me if I liked him, and I said I didn't even know him. She just gave me a weird smile, you know? And then she pretended to be my friend for three days. I should have known she didn't mean it because eventually she'd always go off with her friends, and I wouldn't be included. I was just so desperate for friends. It was pathetic." The pain in her voice was raw, and he knew there had to be more than the friend dropping her.

"What did the boy have to do with it?" he asked warily.

"Nothing. Well, nothing to me, but she was in love with him, and she talked a lot about how I thought she could get him to notice her. She's in a film class, and she wanted to interview me, and I told her about my old friends and my old boyfriend back in St. Louis, but she cut it all up and pasted it back so it looked like I was in love with the boy. She even had some scenes I didn't know she'd taken, with me suggesting things she could do to win him—only she made it look like I had already done all that. And I barely knew his name!"

"Man, I'm sorry." Garth shook his head in sympathy. "I'm guessing she sent it to him?"

"Worse. She put it on the student news that we watch in school every morning. Now everyone believes I'm passionately in love with him and that we're having some kind of thing. She even filmed us talking in the lunchroom that one time. All the shots of me are awful. I look . . . so ugly and fat—really terrible. And it turns out he had a girlfriend, who broke up with him because of it. Now he's mad at me, and everyone else is also mad—or laughing at me. It's even all over social media. I just want to roll up in a ball and die!" She pulled her knees to her chest and wrapped her arms around them, turning her head to face the window, but not before he glimpsed tears sliding down her cheek.

Fury filled him, but he fought it down enough to ask, "And your mom talked to the principal?"

A huge sniff met his question, and then, "Yeah. The girl was suspended for three days, but not really for what she did to me. It was for exchanging the video clip without her teacher's permission. Student work has to be approved, and she changed it after he approved another video she did."

"Well, I guess that's something. What about an apology?"

Cora snorted. "Not a chance. The principal is her mother, and the suspension is a joke. I saw her at school on the last day she was supposed to be suspended, working on her routine in the hallway with the other cheerleaders. She's the real snake, but everyone thinks I'm the terrible one. Mom says it'll blow over, but it won't. Those girls are too mean to let it die. So I'm not going back. Not ever!"

He hadn't been around Cora much as a teen, but he recognized real suffering when he saw it. This wasn't a minor incident of bullying. What was Ivy thinking, sending her back to a place that was obviously unsafe for her?

He reached out a tentative hand to Cora's back, patting it gently. "Thanks for telling me."

She turned, grabbing his hand with a death grip. "Please don't make me go back."

He glanced away from the road to see her pleading eyes, glittering with tears illuminated by the light from the dash. "I'll talk to your mom and see what we can work out. I'm sure she'll understand how it's been for you now." If Ivy didn't already grasp the reality, he'd somehow make her understand. "But how did you get the bus ticket in the first place?"

She released her hold, a tiny smile hovering around her mouth. "I paid a friend cash to buy it online for me so Mom wouldn't be able to find me before I got here. They didn't even ask for ID."

He had to laugh at that. "Good thinking."

The rest of the drive was quiet as Cora dozed, and Garth tried to go over in his head what to do. Ivy wouldn't let Cora go to Florida with him for school, but maybe if he lived in Missouri for a year, close to her, they could work something out temporarily.

But what about Maggie? At the thought, he felt torn. She wouldn't leave Forgotten, would she? No. She was obviously happy there. Besides, whatever had pushed her away from him seemed alive and flourishing, which might mean they had little chance of changing anything between them.

Lapsing into sort of a coma, he drove the rest of the way to Forgotten, rousing Cora when they arrived and helping her up the outside stairs at the café.

"Dad," she murmured as he fumbled with the keys. "I'm really hungry."

"When was the last time you ate?" He should have asked before, back in Lincoln when they might have found a store that was open all night.

She shrugged. "When we changed busses, I got stuff from a vending machine. That's all I ate today."

"Okay, let's get you into the room, and I'll see what I can do." Would Maggie mind if he raided the kitchen for party leftovers? Should he wake her when he knew she'd have to be up in a few hours? No, that thought only came from his selfish desire to see her.

These thoughts fled as he opened the door to his room and found that someone had pulled out a trundle from under the queen bed. Sheets and blankets matching the off-white of the main bed were already on the trundle, ready for sleeping. While Cora beelined for the bathroom, he read a note taped on the mini fridge:

In case you two are hungry after your adventure, I've put some food in here for you. Plates and cutlery are on top of the microwave. I hope everything is okay.
   –Maggie.

Emotions welled inside him. He remembered so many times when he'd come home from work to find that Ivy had left him something to eat. He also remembered the day when her kindness had ceased—years before their marriage had ended.

"Is everything okay?"

He looked up to see Cora standing in the bathroom door, frowning at him. He scrubbed a finger and thumb over his eyes, blotting the moisture. "Just tired. But guess what? We're in luck. The bed and breakfast owner left us some food." His eyes went to the trundle. "And an extra bed."

"Cool."

They ate everything Maggie had left, with Cora inhaling most of it. She hadn't been teasing about her hunger. Afterward, she changed into pajamas, brushed her teeth with a new toothbrush Ivy would be happy to know she'd brought along, and fell asleep in the trundle.

Garth dimmed the lights and went about his own nightly ritual. Finally in bed, he glanced down at Cora on the trundle, feeling a stark loss at the years he hadn't been allowed to be a real part of her life. Maybe that was over now. If only Ivy would bend a little.

His last thoughts, however, were about Maggie and the heirloom pocket watch she still obviously treasured. The watch meant there was hope, even if Cora's presence complicated matters. He wasn't giving up yet.

CHAPTER 13

The next morning, Maggie did her work as her mind wandered. She had awakened in the night with the soft creaks coming from the hallway that told her Garth had made it back to the Butter Cake. She hoped he hadn't been offended that she'd gone into his room, even though he'd indicated on his registration that he preferred only weekly housekeeping. Most of her guests chose that option because it was less expensive, and she preferred it as well since it reduced her workload—normally they didn't stay long enough to make it the whole week. When she heard nothing more, she closed her eyes, utterly exhausted from the day.

Meanwhile, even after only two days without Hannah's full-time help, she was falling behind in her daily tasks. She needed to hire a new employee—and fast. She'd learned enough about burning the candle at both ends, and she didn't want to fall into that habit. Again. Nothing was worth that—not the café or her music.

Not that her music was an issue. Yet even as she had the thought, the words to the song flittered through her mind: *This feeling for you took me by surprise. Makes me question who I am and who I want to be . . .*

She vividly remembered struggling over the last verse to make the song happy enough to inspire fans when her own heart was broken twice over. The pictures of Zach had helped. Until he was gone and there were no more pictures. But that was long after the song had topped all the music charts.

She was putting the bread into the oven when she heard the rustle of someone at the counter. She emerged, expecting to find Garth but was surprised instead to see a teenage girl with long brown hair, beautiful blue eyes, and a round, somewhat childish face that featured a tiny rash of pimples across her forehead. Her pale blue T-shirt bore the sketch of a horse, and the denim jeans were fashionably ripped. She looked infinitely sad.

"Good morning," Maggie said, injecting cheer into the words. "You must be Cora."

She nodded. "I hope it's okay I'm down here. My dad's asleep, and I got bored upstairs. I practically slept all day on the bus yesterday."

"I'm glad you came down," Maggie said. "I bet you're hungry. Why don't you come into the kitchen with me?"

"Okay."

Maggie gestured for her to sit at the little table while she made up a plate of bacon, eggs, and hash browns, placing them in front of the teen.

"Bacon." The girl sighed. "I really shouldn't. All that fat."

Maggie smiled as she placed a glass of whole milk in front of the girl. "Trust me. If you eat good foods regularly with a decent amount of fat, you won't feel as inclined to fill up on sweets.

Sure, nuts and avocados might be better fats, but a little bacon won't hurt. As you can see, the hash browns are the only carbs here, and you'll need those for quick energy." She set a fruit bowl next to the milk. "And a little fruit goes a long way toward sugar cravings."

"Really?" Cora said.

"I think so." Maggie lowered her voice as if confiding a secret. "But you still need to have a piece of my butter cake sometime today."

"I wish I looked like you," Cora mumbled, picking up a piece of bacon with her fingers.

"Why?" Maggie asked. "You're beautiful exactly the way you are. And I think you'll only grow more so as you get older. You have good lines."

For the first time, Cora's smile was real. She picked up her fork and stabbed a bit of egg. "Who are you anyway? You kind of look familiar."

Maggie sat in the chair opposite her. "I'm Maggie Tremblay." She extended her hand to shake Cora's. As the girl reached out, she noticed a horseshoe ring on her finger that matched the silver necklace she wore. "I own this café. And we've actually met, but you were only three at the time, so I doubt you remember."

"But . . ." Cora's brow creased. "So you know my dad."

"Yeah. It was a long time ago, though. You might have seen pictures." They'd posed for some at the base, and Garth also had two pictures from the photo booth they'd ducked into in Trenton—if he still had them. She'd burned her own matching set after singing at the base.

"That's probably it." Cora began eating again. "I looked up Forgotten on my phone. Where I live now is a small town, but this place is really tiny. I wondered why he would be here, but it makes sense for him to stop in if he knows you. I mean, it's not like there's an airport here where he could work."

Maggie nodded. "True. The size of the town is part of what I love about Forgotten. Everyone knows everyone else, and newcomers are welcome, no matter where you're from. In fact, local legend says most people who come to Forgotten temporarily because they want to leave behind their pasts end up finding themselves and staying."

Cora's eyes widened as if the words struck a chord in her. "Is that what happened to you?"

"Something like that. I found the café online and loved the exterior, but once I came here and walked down Main Street, I knew it was home."

"I would love to forget," Cora said, talking through a mouthful of eggs. "Too bad I can't stay here, but my mom wouldn't let me."

"What does your mom do?"

"She manages an office supply store. Boring." Cora rolled her eyes. "Anyway, maybe she'll let me go to Florida."

"To live with Garth?"

"Right. It's not like I could have lived with him before now because he was overseas so much, but now that he's retired, things could be different." She heaved a sigh. "I just want to be eighteen already. Then I wouldn't need my mom to agree."

More questions filled Maggie's mind, but she'd done enough prying. "Well, I'd better go start the coffee and turn over the closed sign. It's almost seven. Would you like anything else before I do that?"

"No," Cora said, picking up her last piece of bacon. "But I can help if you want. I work at a Subway back home. Besides, I don't want to go back upstairs. I'll have to call my mom."

Maggie chuckled, glad that Garth was making her face the

music. "I actually could use a hand. I lost an employee this week. Someone's coming in at ten-thirty, but yesterday it was a madhouse before that. Your dad even pitched in. You should have seen him in my yellow apron."

"Really?" Cora laughed. "I would have loved to see that. I mean, his omelets are great, but I can't imagine him in one of those aprons."

"Speaking of which." Maggie took one off the hook by the door and tossed it to her. Cora wasn't wearing a white blouse, but her blue tee would do.

"Cool."

An hour later, Maggie was coming out of the kitchen with a tray of three breakfasts when Garth slid onto a stool at the counter where Cora was ringing up an order. He was dressed in jeans and a navy shirt, and his hair was still wet and mussed as if he'd hurried to get ready.

"Look," Cora said to him, pulling out a small wad of folded cash. "I already earned a few bucks."

"Good for you." Garth's gaze went past her to Maggie, who felt heat rise to her face. "Thank you for taking care of her."

"Oh, no, she's definitely helping *me*. We had a rush right when we opened, but we've slowed down now, so any time you need to take her . . ."

"First, you need to order." Cora held up a pad. "What do you want?"

"I'll have an omelet," he said, grinning. "With a side of pickles."

A tremor ran through Maggie's stomach at his words.

"Ooh, gross." Cora glanced at Maggie. "Do you even do that?"

"We try to accommodate everything reasonable, and pickles are easy. But you don't need to ring up your dad. Since he's staying here, breakfast is always on the house."

Cora's shoulders slumped. "Rats. Guess that means no tip."

Garth pulled out a five-dollar bill. "You can have this if I can eat in the kitchen. I've got a headache, and my definition of busy doesn't seem to be the same as Maggie's." He looked around at the occupied tables meaningfully.

"Come on back," Maggie told him, laughing as Cora grabbed the bill. "Guess sometimes there's such a thing as a little too much friendliness in Forgotten."

Garth pointed at Cora. "The minute you get a break, come back here. Your mom has already called me this morning."

Cora made a face but nodded. "Okay." She motioned to a table of people. "I gotta give them their bill first."

Back in the kitchen, Maggie whipped up an omelet, which apparently lived up to Garth's standards, if she judged by the eager way he downed it.

"I'm sorry if she got in the way," he said.

"She didn't. Like I said, she's been helping. And I'm glad you found her."

"She was at the bus station in Lincoln. She paid a friend to buy her a ticket online. That's why they couldn't trace her." He frowned. "I'm hoping we can work things out with her mother, because quite frankly, I'm on Cora's side. She shouldn't have to go back to that high school."

"Do I even dare ask what happened?" Maggie began frying more bacon.

"No, because I can't tell you, except to say that it was bullying, and I don't believe it'll be a safe place for her. Time will tell if Ivy comes to that same conclusion."

"I'm sorry. It's a tough world out there. Sometimes I feel we're very protected here in Forgotten. When bullying happens in our schools, the kids have to work for the mayor himself as a kind of community service. He's good at changing their attitudes. But we're small enough here to do that. Several smaller towns nearby bus their middle schoolers and high school kids here for their education, but there are not a lot of students."

"In Cora's case, it's the principal's kid doing the bullying."

Maggie slid a few pieces of bacon onto his plate. "That's too bad. I'm glad you're fighting for her."

"Whatever I do, it's Ivy who has to make the decision." Resignation colored his voice.

A flare of irritation pierced Maggie's heart. Couldn't he go to court? Couldn't he do something more? But she bit her tongue as Cora came into the kitchen, her phone pressed against her ear.

"No, Mom," she was saying. "Nothing happened. Julie's cousins were nice people. They didn't know I was running away." She paused, listening. "You know why. It's never going to get better." Another pause as defiance slid over Cora's round face. "No way. I'm not going back to that school. Not ever. Does it matter to you if I'd rather slit my own wrists?"

Maggie exchanged a look with Garth, her concern growing.

"Please, Mom," Cora begged. Another long pause and then a smile came over her face. "Really? Okay. Thank you. Yeah. I love you too." Cora hung up and ran the few remaining steps to Garth, flinging her arms around his neck. "Thank you, thank you, thank you! You're the best ever."

Garth chuckled, meeting Maggie's gaze over Cora's shoulder. "What she means is we'll be staying here until Saturday afternoon or evening, depending on available flights. If that's okay with you."

"Of course." But Maggie couldn't help thinking about Connor. Hadn't he mentioned something about Saturday? She'd have to text him to say it wouldn't work this weekend because she couldn't leave the café for long with guests here, especially when she was down an employee. Besides, she really didn't want them together under the same roof. If Connor came on Sunday instead like usual, Garth would be gone and her life would proceed as normal. That was what she wanted, wasn't it?

Cora pulled away from Garth, grinning. "I know Saturday isn't far off. But right now it feels like forever," she said.

"You two should go to the reservoir or do something else," Maggie suggested. "And I bet tomorrow I could arrange a horseback ride for Cora, if she's interested."

Cora's eyes widened. "I would *love* that! How did you know?"

"Your shirt and ring and necklace. In fact, one of my teen employees who works here has horses."

Cora's hand went to her necklace. "Is she going to be here today?"

"Yep. She used to work only weekends, but since we have so many construction workers in town at the moment, she's been working more often, and now that I've lost an employee, she'll be here every day for two or three hours after school."

"That's cool. I bet your high school is really small."

"Yep, but the kids are all really great. If you're around later, you might meet some of them."

"Cool."

Quiet fell over the kitchen. "We could go fishing at the reservoir," Garth said.

Cora wrinkled her nose. "I'd rather go swimming."

He laughed. "You brought a suit?"

"Duh. Of course. I looked up Forgotten on the Internet. Besides all the fairs and community events, the lake is like . . . well, their best attraction."

"Except I didn't bring a swimming suit."

"So go buy one while I help Maggie." Cora peeked out the kitchen door. "More people. I'll get them."

Garth burst into laughter as she darted away. "Okay then," he said to Maggie. "Is there anywhere I can buy a swimsuit?"

"Joni's dress shop down the street. It's owned by Natalie McColl."

"Who?"

"The Police Chief's wife, the birthday girl you met last night." At his nod, she added, "They could still have a few suits, though it's late in the season. If not, you might have to drive to Panna Creek to the Walmart and look through their clearance. That's about all we got."

"Sounds promising. If worse comes to worst, I'll go in my jeans."

Maggie nodded, their eyes locking. Abruptly, she was all too aware of his presence and of the unspoken words between them. The intensity of his stare seemed to reach into the very core of who she was. She had to force herself back to work and was relieved when he quickly finished his breakfast and left by the kitchen door.

When Keisha showed up to work, Cora came back into the kitchen. "It's dead now," she said. "I guess that means it's break time." She laughed. "This is so much better than Subway. I'm glad I came here."

"I'm glad you did too." Maggie turned from the soup she'd finished putting together. She was glad to see Cora feeling happier than earlier this morning, and if not telling Garth about Zach's sickness had contributed to Cora's happiness as a child, maybe withholding the information had been the right thing to do. But would Garth see it that way?

"Want to learn how to make butter cake?" Maggie asked her. "At least until your dad gets back?"

"Sure. Can I taste some?"

"Absolutely. How about we first pack a lunch with some cake for you and your dad? There are a few pans of it in the display out front. But choose from the right side. It's best aged at least twenty-four hours, and the older ones are always on the right."

"Okay."

They packed a lunch of sandwiches and butter cake, and then they shared an extra piece of cake.

"This is wonderful!" Cora gushed. "How can you stand not eating it all day?"

Maggie laughed. "Well, you learn to pace yourself."

Cora stopped eating, falling silent as she stared at her fork. "I really wish I could stay longer than Saturday. Because my mom won't let me go to Florida with Garth—I asked and she said no—so it would be nice to at least hang out here another week."

Garth? Since when did the child call her father by his first name? Hadn't she said Dad before? Maggie couldn't remember.

"You live with your mother full time?" Maggie already knew this, and she hated herself a little for prying. She usually tried to stay away from participating in the nosey gossip that was common in Forgotten.

"Well, yeah, and with my dad until they got divorced last month." Cora's jaw clenched and unclenched. "Then Mom put me in an awful school. That's why I came to find Garth."

"You call him Garth? Isn't he your father?" There Maggie was, prying again.

Cora set down her fork. "Well, he is, but not my birth father. My mom married him when I was two because my dad was a total jerk. And to be honest, he never really changed. I don't know why my mom ever went back to him."

The words stole Maggie's breath, and she found herself clutching at the table. That meant Cora was Garth's stepdaughter, and he hadn't been married during their email courtship as she'd assumed after singing at his Air Force base in Texas. It also meant her decision to withhold information about his son on those grounds was unjustified. And if Maggie had given him her contact information in Trenton, maybe he would have returned to her . . . and Zach. Maybe he would have been by her side when their son slipped from this world.

"Are you okay?" Cora was staring at her.

"Just thinking," Maggie said, struggling to keep her voice even and her emotions from her face. "That's got to be hard. I know what it's like to have a father let me down." She forced a smile. No wonder Garth didn't have custody of Cora. She'd been judging him for that too.

"Well, I consider Garth my *real* dad, the kind that counts, but I guess I got out of the habit of calling him Dad since they've been divorced so long. But I'm going to call him that again since my other dad isn't around to get mad at me now when I say it."

Maggie could imagine the problems that would have caused. "Well, let's get to making some new butter cake while we're slow. I suspect your dad had to drive to Panna Creek."

She let routine take over, but for the second day in a row, she didn't remember putting in the cake ingredients. If she'd been wrong about so much, what else had she been wrong about?

Maybe the heartaches of the past weren't Garth's fault but all her own.

CHAPTER 14

Later that afternoon, Garth and Cora returned to the Butter Cake Café at six o'clock, slightly burnt but happy. They'd tried out the pizza place in town for dinner, mostly because he was concerned about all the extra food Maggie was giving them. He hadn't come here to be a burden to her, especially when she was short-handed.

Excited to go down to the dining room and meet Ingrid and learn about her horses, Cora claimed the first shower. She was out the door before Garth could make it from the desk chair to the bathroom. She looked happy and content. Nothing like the sullen teenager she'd been on his last visit. Somehow, he had to convince Ivy to let her try a year with him, even if it meant moving to Missouri. He could work part time as a pilot over the weekends when she was with Ivy and be home for her after school during the week. His retirement wage from the Air Force made that possible, and he could even pick up non-flying work in the mornings if needed.

Still running through options in his head, he went downstairs to find Cora sitting on a stool next to Maggie on the customer side of the counter, listening to an eager Ingrid talking about her horses. Cora popped up when she saw him. "Can I go riding with Ingrid tonight? She exercises her horses every night. She has a horse I can use."

"I don't know," he hedged. "You've only ridden twice before." The last time was when he'd taken her himself during an all-day visit last year. They'd learned how to saddle and groom, but the actual riding had only been about three hours.

"Anyone can ride Sunny," Ingrid said, her freckled face crinkling in a grin. "Even my baby sister, and she's only five."

"Please, Dad," Cora begged.

"I promise to take good care of her," Ingrid added.

Garth looked to Maggie, whose shrug told him he was on his own. "Can I come to see?" Garth held his breath, waiting for Cora to roll her eyes and complain about his protectiveness, but it was Ingrid who spoke.

"That would be great," she said. "You can watch us for a while in the field so you can see how gentle Sunny is. Plus, I still want to hear about those medals you won."

Cora bounced a little on her seat. "Oh, he has really cool stories. One time, his plane was shot down, and he had to make an emergency landing. He saved everyone on board, and he got the supplies to the soldiers and helped them win the battle before stealing an enemy plane and saving the wounded, even though he was wounded himself. They gave him the medal of honor and a purple heart for that one."

A fleeting protest rose to Garth's tongue—he was proud of that medal, but it sounded more heroic coming from her lips when in reality it had been terror, blood, and adrenaline that had kept them all going. Plus, he certainly hadn't been the only hero that day.

"It was a tough time," he said, hoping that would be the end of it.

"You know what?" Maggie said, her eyes knowing. "Why don't you all go now? It looks like the dinner rush is over already, and we'll be closing soon anyway."

"Cool." Ingrid started removing her apron.

"You should go too," Keisha said to Maggie, coming from a table with an armful of plates. "Lisa and I can finish up. You've been here all day."

Garth looked at Maggie, noting weariness in her face that he'd been too preoccupied to see before. No wonder she was sitting down at the counter. She tilted her head to the side as if considering.

"I'd like you to come," he said. "We haven't had a lot of time to catch up." Did her face pale at the words? He wasn't sure.

Maggie's gaze went from him to Keisha and then to Cora. "Okay," she said, her chin lifting slightly. "I'll need to change."

That was how twenty minutes later, they found themselves at Ingrid's family farm, watching her show Cora how to drive a horse around in an outdoor corral made from rough-hewn tree logs. Finally, they saddled the animal, and Cora swung up into the saddle, riding around the ring all on her own, beaming as brightly as she had the day he'd taught her to ride a bike. Nostalgia for the child she'd been clogged his throat. So many years he'd lost out on with her since the divorce.

No, he couldn't think that way, or the old resentment would eat him alive.

"She'll be okay." Maggie touched his arm.

"They grow up so fast."

His comment seemed to sadden her. "Yeah. But she seems like a sweet girl."

"Mostly. She does have a bristly side and sometimes a pretty foul mouth, something I won't tolerate because I want her to be heard, not dismissed. Right now, I think she's on her best behavior." His eyes dropped to her lips, a movement she noted because her face clearly flushed. His heart pounded in answer.

"She wants to live with you?"

He nodded. "Her mother will never let her, though. At least not in Florida, and maybe not anywhere else. But I have to do something to help her. I'm not sure what." The girls had left the corral and were now heading across the field away from them.

"We'll be back in less than an hour," shouted Ingrid over her shoulder.

Garth chuckled. "Looks like they got it under control. That horse does seem rather docile. Should we go for a walk?"

"Sure." Maggie's voice was casual, but a hardness had come over her face, as if she dreaded being alone with him. So much for starting a new past.

They walked across a field toward a little trail that led to a large copse of trees. "You know," he said as they followed the path, "I got flack for years for losing that pocket watch."

Her face relaxed slightly. "You did?"

"Yep. I told you it was my great grandpa's, but what I didn't tell you—what I didn't know at the time—is that it's solid gold, a family heirloom. My dad was not happy." He chuckled to show it didn't bother him.

She smiled with him. "I'm so sorry. I did learn that it was gold when I tried to find a chain for it before I moved here—the jeweler said I needed a gold chain that wasn't harder than the gold of the watch itself, so it wouldn't wear the loop connecting them. Before that, I kept it in my jewelry box. I did wonder at your giving me such a valuable piece, but . . ." Maggie shrugged and hesitated a few seconds before adding, "I can give it back to you."

"No, please, keep it. I gave it to you, and my father has long forgiven me." Taking it back now didn't seem right.

They'd reached the trees, the path cutting between verdant bushes and wild grasses. They walked another few yards, the tension less between them now, but he was no closer to the truth.

"Look," he said, "I'm sorry if you feel I've been too pushy since I got here. I didn't come to make your life miserable. I came because . . . well, seeing you singing that song after so many years, I couldn't not come." Those were his words she'd put in the song, the ones he'd used to propose. Did she even remember that part of their past?

Maggie sighed, her hand going out to pluck at a bush they were passing. "To tell you the truth, I'm not sure what I'm feeling. Your coming here . . . you have to understand, I once wished more than anything that you would find me, and then when you did . . . it was too late. Not your fault, but I blamed you."

He stopped walking and faced her. Tears glittered in her eyes, wetting her dark lashes. He wanted to take her into his arms and kiss her until the tears were nothing more than a memory, but that wouldn't solve anything right now. He had to understand. "I'm sorry I took so long to find your contact info, but you didn't make it easy."

"I know. That was my fault. I didn't believe what I felt between us. I couldn't trust that it was real. And I didn't want to wait for a soldier."

"Because of your father, right?" He remembered the tense-ness in her voice when she'd told him the story of her mother's relationship with another US airman, and he'd seen how much her father's abandonment had hurt her. "I wish I'd somehow convinced you that I wasn't like him."

"It was more because of my mother. I didn't want to be like her—complaining about the man who'd wronged her, barely scraping by, becoming an alcoholic. Grumbling about how much of a burden I was on her because of him. But yes, I also didn't want any future child of mine to grow up without a father."

The words pierced him, though he knew they were more about her than him. "I would never abandon my child."

"I know that now." Maggie dropped her gaze, and a tear fell to her cheek.

"So we both made mistakes," he said into the silence. "But I think there's still something here between us. Maybe we should give it a chance. Tell me it's not only in my imagination."

"It's not." The words were encouraging, but she still wouldn't look at him. He stepped closer, reaching for her, but her hands came up, warding him off. "There's more."

He entwined his fingers with hers. "Then tell me. I can understand why you were so careful in Trenton, but once I found you . . . after those months of emails . . . why did you stop? You don't know how much your emails meant to me. I loved you, Maggie. What happened?"

Slowly her face came up, her eyes meeting his. Another tear slipped down her cheek, testing his control. "When you asked me to sing at the base, I planned to tell you everything that day—what I'd done and why I'd broken things off. But then I met your wife and daughter, and I realized she would have been expecting when we were exchanging those emails."

"You thought I'd cheated on you." A pit opened in his gut.

Maggie shrugged. "It didn't matter by then, not really. I was engaged, and you had Ivy. You were happy. You had a family. You didn't need the past coming back to haunt you." She stopped talking, her eyes searching his.

Searching for what? Forgiveness? He couldn't tell. "I knew the minute I saw you at the base that I wasn't over you," he said. In truth, seeing her then had made him wonder how he'd ever gone on with his life.

A slight nod made his hopes soar. "I hadn't expected to still feel that way when I saw you either. That's why I didn't marry Axel, even though I knew you and I could never be together. It wasn't fair to him. So I came here and started over. But I didn't ruin things for you, did I?"

"No. Not at all. After that day, I tried harder to make my marriage work." Somehow it was important to make her understand that. "But in the end, Ivy wanted things I couldn't give her." Mostly she'd wanted him to quit flying, which meant giving up a large part of who he had become. Having another child had also become an obsession with her, one he'd simply been unable to fill.

Maggie started to loosen her fingers from his, but he tightened his grip, pulling one of her hands to his cheek. "Why did you break up with me?"

Her breathing came faster, not fueled by desire but panic. What had happened to make her fear him so much?

"Please," he said. "I won't hurt you."

A sob escaped her throat. "My heart is already broken, and I don't think it can ever be fixed."

"What?" Confusion washed over him. Was she talking about his marrying Ivy or something else?

Her next words came at him like a bullet. "I had a son." She wrenched away from him, her hand going to the pocket watch and dragging it out from under her blue plaid blouse. She pulled the chain over her head and clicked the watch open, handing it to him. "*We* had a son. I placed him for adoption."

A son? He could barely understand the words. Her face was so earnest, but her eyes were terrible and lost. He looked down at the watch in his hand, where a picture nestled inside the top half, an image of a little boy not more than a few years old.

A son. A son. A son.

The words reverberated inside his skull. The child would have been conceived that magical day in Trenton when they'd both fallen so hard, and excitement, thrill, and passion had overcome every other emotion. He'd fathered a child. He was both horrified and amazed. Horrified that all his choices had been taken away, and amazed that somewhere out there was a person with his blood coursing inside his veins. Ivy had been wrong about his ability to father a child.

"His name is Zach," Maggie continued softly.

Zach. That was Garth's father's name. No way the name hadn't been intentional.

"I placed him for adoption before you found me again. He's why I stopped sending messages. I knew there couldn't be a life between us without our son."

He could feel her gaze on him, but he couldn't take his eyes from the picture. "Where is he? He's a little older than Cora now, right? Does he live nearby? Do you ever see him?" Maybe that was the real reason she'd moved here.

When there was no response, he dragged his gaze to Maggie's. Her upper teeth bit into her lower lip, but that didn't stop its quivering as she fought tears.

"No," she said, her voice faint and full of pain. "Zach contracted a severe form of leukemia. That's what I went to tell you at the base. He wasn't going to make it, and I thought you might want to say goodbye."

"Goodbye?" All the visions Garth had been building in his mind these past few moments burst into a flash of burning ruin.

She nodded. "His adoptive parents and I tried everything—chemo, radiation. They used my bone marrow for a transplant, but nothing worked." Her face crumpled as the tears came in earnest. "I failed him. He died. That's the real reason I stopped singing and came to Forgotten."

His anger flared, overriding his urge to comfort her. "You should have told me!"

"You think so?" Her voice was hard again. "Really? Because I was going to until I saw you and realized it was selfish of me. You'd gone on with your life. You were happy. You had a wife and a child. Zach . . . he wouldn't mean to you what he meant to me anyway, so why should I put you through that heartache?"

How could she say such a horrible thing? Could she really believe that because he had a wife and child he wouldn't feel for a son who had been kept from him?

"Of course I went on," he ground out. "I had no other choice. You *gave* me no other choice, remember?"

"I thought I was saving you pain!" More tears ran down her cheeks. "Watching Zach waste away and die was the worst thing that ever happened to me."

He steeled himself against her pain. "I should have been there. You had no right to keep my son from me."

They glared at each other for long minutes. Garth's hands fisted at his side, one still holding the pocket watch, while Maggie's arms folded protectively over her abdomen. Her arms were a barrier between them—like his anger.

"I made the hardest decision a woman alone could ever make," she said finally, this time her voice steady and devoid of emotion. "I had no choice, either."

"You could have contacted the base in Trenton. They would have been able to track down my unit in Afghanistan."

"And then what? Wait for you to come home? Like my mother waited for my father? I barely knew you. I wasn't going to trust my son's future to you."

"You did know me!" He jabbed a finger in the direction of her heart. "We connected here, like no one else ever did. You just won't admit it. And for the last time, I am nothing like your father." The words came out like gravel grinding in his throat.

Maggie wiped the tears from her face. "I've regretted not telling you my entire life. If I had to do it over, I'd make different decisions, starting with not sleeping with you." Her voice was still steady, but her dark eyes flashed anger. "I was barely a year older than Cora. Think of that! I made the only choices I could for who I was then. And don't you ever doubt that I did everything I could for our son. For the four short years of his life, he had the best parents any child could have. They did everything possible to save him."

Her words only infuriated him further. "*I* was his father. *I* deserved to know." He'd had a son all along, one he would never be able to hold. One he would never teach to throw a ball. He didn't know what to do with the incredible loss he felt.

"I know," she said in almost a whisper. "I'm sorry."

"Sorry doesn't cut it." Anger roiled inside him, and it was only his training that allowed him to clamp his mouth shut on the rest of the hurtful words he wanted to fling at her.

She nodded slowly. "And that's why there's no way of rewriting the past." She turned her back on him and started through the trees. He stared after her, not knowing what to do. Before his frozen mind came to a conclusion, she was already gone.

At once the anger seeped from him, leaving his legs weak and his stomach nauseated. Funny how when faced with enemy fighter jets, he'd found the courage to run at them head-on, decimating the enemy. How when plummeting to the ground after being hit, he'd somehow had the strength of mind to stop and restart the engines in time to make an emergency crash landing. He'd been able to tourniquet his own leg and walk miles to deliver supplies. With a hole in his chest, he'd stolen an enemy plane and gotten his crew to safety.

But news of a son he'd never known paralyzed him. He couldn't control his raging thoughts, his deep sense of loss. He couldn't call out or take a step.

He couldn't stop Maggie from leaving.

Again.

He slumped to the ground, elbows on knees, head in his hands, and wept.

CHAPTER 15

Maggie had known from the beginning that Garth would regret coming to Forgotten. In retrospect, she should have prepared him better for the news, but it was too late now. Part of her was relieved to have it out in the open. Maybe she could finally begin her own life, starting with a husband and another child—in that order this time.

Another part of her, the part that thrilled every time Garth looked at her, was devastated that he hadn't taken her in his arms and told her he understood the horrors she'd been through. She ached at his accusation of withholding his son—which she had, of course, so she deserved his hatred. She'd thought the anguish of losing Zach, of losing Garth, was in the past. But here that grief was, as fresh as when she'd sobbed in Delitra's arms all those years ago.

Tears blocked her vision as she went through the trees. She knew the area well enough, so there was no chance of getting lost. The river was nearby, and that was where she'd go, to soothe her feet and her heart.

In a few minutes, she reached one of the neighborhood swimming holes along the river, where children had pulled up dirt and built up a rock dam to collect the water. The flow was low this time of year, but the hole was full. She kicked off her sandals, rolled up the bottoms of her capris, and lowered herself to the grassy bank, plunging in her feet and gasping slightly at the coldness.

A blink sent several more tears down her cheeks, but she was already recovering. "*I'm okay,*" she told Zach, her hand going to the spot between her breasts. But the pocket watch wasn't there. She clenched her lips tightly against a sob that threatened to break through her calm. The watch was Garth's, and she had other pictures of Zach. Maybe letting go of the watch was the final act of healing.

If only she could convince herself.

After a time of staring blankly at the rushing waters and feeling her feet go numb, thoughts of the café entered her mind. She needed to get back to make sure tomorrow's preparations were all ready.

She texted Charlotte: *Are you busy? I'm at the swimming hole between the Pattersons' and Whitings' right now and need a ride back to the café. I'll walk to the Whitings' after I get my shoes on. It's not an emergency, though, so only come if you're free.*

Having Charlotte pick her up at the Whitings' house meant Maggie wouldn't have to return to Ingrid's and risk facing Garth again tonight. If Charlotte didn't answer, Maggie would still go over to the Whitings' and ask for a ride back to the Butter Cake Café. Terrell Whiting owned the grocery store on Main, across from the city park, and she was good friends with both him and his wife. They would be happy to help, and she'd been meaning to gift them a loaf of bread anyway. Terrel often depended on her for freshly made food since his wife, one of the sweetest women Maggie knew, burned everything she cooked.

On my way, Charlotte texted a moment later.

Relieved that she wouldn't have to make up an excuse for the Whitings, Maggie lay back on the grass. Her face was in the shade of the trees, but her body lay in the light still cast by the nearly setting sun. Her feet were icy in the water. It was a study of differences as the change of seasons approached. Colder nights were coming soon.

She knew she should get up and walk to the Whitings. Still, she remained, her feet cool, her body warmed and cocooned by the day's heat radiating from the ground. She let herself drift in the earthy aroma of the riverbank.

She'd been wrong about Garth, and now it really was too late. She'd seen the fury and disbelief in his eyes. Her stomach felt heavy at the thought, and the lack of the chain around her neck made her feel unanchored, as if there were nothing keeping her on earth. Even her café seemed far removed, as did the people of Forgotten, her new family.

A slight rustle was all the warning she had before something soft hit her chest. "Hey, Sleeping Beauty," Charlotte said, sitting beside her. "I'm here."

Maggie's eyes opened as she sat up, pulling her frozen feet from the water. "Good, a towel." She used it to dry her feet. "Sorry. I lost track of time. We can go now." She started to rise, but Charlotte's hand stopped her.

"Or we can stay. What happened?" Charlotte's gaze searched her face, her eyes a vibrant green that seemed to soak up the color of the grass. "You told him, didn't you?"

Maggie nodded. "It didn't go well. He was angry, and I don't blame him. When I found out he was married, I assumed he'd played me during our long-distance email whatever-it-was, but he wasn't married, and his daughter is his stepdaughter. He wasn't married at the time we cyber dated. I made a mistake. Another one."

Charlotte squeezed her hand. "You did what you thought was right."

"I excluded him. I basically told him he wasn't worthy of knowing Zach."

"You couldn't have known, and whatever he thinks now, you saved him and his family pain then."

"Until now."

Charlotte studied her with concern. "Look, you did the right thing telling him. Now he knows, and you can both go on with your lives."

"Yeah, but he came here because he thought we might have a chance at finding what we lost. If he'd known, he probably wouldn't have come." Pain echoed through Maggie's heart. "And so help me, every time I see his face, every time I look into his eyes, I want . . . I want . . ." *Him.* She wanted Garth—and their dreams and everything they'd shared in Trenton. But except for that first day, everything else had been based upon lies—her lies. "It's my fault. I should have chosen differently." She stared at her hands, gripping her knees so tightly her flesh turned white.

Charlotte made a sound in her throat that was more a growl than anything else. Maggie jerked her gaze toward her friend in time to see her squaring her shoulders, a disapproving frown on her face. "You know better than that, Maggie Tremblay. You can't change the past any more than I can change that I didn't go to nursing school, or that Keisha could take back getting hit by a car, or her uncle could return and change his decision to marry that horrid Olivia. Ronica can't change the fact of her husband's dementia, and Chief McColl can't change his daughter's drug abuse. Things happen to all of us. We make mistakes."

Maggie nodded. "I know that." So many of their friends had endured heartaches, yet they went on. So had she, but how could she go on from this seemingly boundless pain breaking her heart all over again?

"You've done what you can. If this ends it between you and Garth, then at least you can go forward with Connor or one of those lawyers who keeps coming into the café. Or someone else new. You've paid the price."

"My price for failing." Maggie gave her a thin smile.

"No." Charlotte made a chopping motion. "You didn't fail anyone. You made choices, things happened, and you paid the consequences. You didn't do any of it from spite. Maybe from hurt, but not from spite. And you certainly didn't fail Zach. He had the best you and his parents could give him. You told me that, and I know it's true."

Maggie sniffed hard. "I do know that. I just . . . if you could have seen his face—he hates me now. Really hates me."

"No, he hates that he didn't know. Give him time to figure the rest out." Charlotte tapped the towel, still in Maggie's lap. "You know what you need? To remember you're alive. And that if Garth walks away, you'll still be alive with a future ahead."

Maggie stared at the towel and then followed Charlotte's gaze to the water. "Are you crazy? It's freezing. My feet are still numb from only a few minutes."

Charlotte laughed. "That never stopped you before. Remember the polar challenge last January at the reservoir? You showed us all up. And I brought the towel in the first place because I was ninety-nine percent certain you'd already jumped in anyway, without even inviting me, I might add. Besides, only the top is flowing with cold water. Underneath, it'll be warmer."

"I'm pretty sure warmer things rise."

"Not the way this dam is built. Come on. You'll see. But better keep your underwear on in case any of the teens ditch their evening chores and show up here. It's not too late in the year for them to swim, even on a school night."

Maggie laughed and jumped to her feet. "You're on. Last one in is a rotten egg."

In answer, Charlotte rose swiftly and pulled her shirt over her head.

Maggie's loose capris were off at the same time as Charlotte's tennis shoes, and her blouse barely before Charlotte's tight jeans. Together, they splashed into the swimming hole, gasping and squealing at the cold. But Charlotte was right that it wasn't as cold in the deeper middle, the water almost motionless between the currents that rushed along the edges.

Maggie moved her arm over the water, sending a spray in Charlotte's direction. Charlotte screamed and shot back. Maggie dunked underneath and splashed Charlotte with her feet, her limbs warming with the exercise. When she came up, Charlotte was ready for her, and Maggie choked on the water splashed in her face.

They tired quickly of the game and floated on their backs, faces to the sky. The sun was now almost completely behind the hills, the clouds it painted radiating orange through the trees. All Maggie's problems faded. This was exactly what she needed. This place, this moment, was enduring. Even when she was gone, this swimming hole would be here, and kids and teens and men and women like her would come here, and life would go on.

"I feel about twelve years old," Maggie said.

"Isn't it great?" Charlotte sighed. "But it turns out I really am freezing." She started swimming toward the bank. "Come on. It'll be dark soon."

Maggie didn't feel cold. She felt alive and tingly. She felt powerful and young and full of possibilities, as if a few decisions hadn't controlled her entire life.

"Next time," Charlotte called from the bank, "let's do this earlier in the day when it's warmer."

"Nothing a little hot chocolate won't cure." Maggie caught the now-damp towel Charlotte tossed at her and began drying off. "But thank you. For everything."

Charlotte pulled on her shirt. "You'll do the same for me when it's my turn. Sometimes it takes a bit of risk to remind us we're alive."

"Not everyone would go into the river with me," Maggie countered. "Guess that's why we're best friends."

Charlotte tilted her head to look at her. "As your best friend, I have one more thing to say. If you really think you might still love Garth, you need to fight for him, even if it means he's who you're fighting against. And even if it means exposing your heart. Because I've never seen you react this way to any man, and this time you don't want any regrets." With a decisive nod, she turned and started off through the trees.

Maggie stared after her friend. Hiding somewhere and licking her wounds sounded a lot more appealing than fighting for anything involving Garth, but what if this was her last chance? She'd thought it was already too late, but maybe Charlotte was right.

She glanced over her shoulder in the direction of the trees where she'd left Garth. Was he still walking around or already on his way back to the café with Cora? Would they be leaving Forgotten tonight? And what would she do if they did?

If he was planning on leaving, she didn't have to make it easy for him. This time, he'd have to be the one to let her go.

CHAPTER 16

G arth needed to vent, or at least to talk everything out with someone, but for the past two months, he'd been severing ties with his Air Force buddies. His family would have been an option if he'd ever told them about Maggie. No, he'd have to work this out for himself. He needed to figure out where to go from here.

At the moment, his world was dark, but he'd lived through enough battles to know it was always darkest before making a choice and pushing forward. Before the action, one could only guess at the outcome, teetering in indecision. Even in his hurt and anger, he knew the outcome between him and Maggie was yet unfinished, undecided.

He had a son Maggie had hidden from him. Was she right that there could be no relationship between them without the child?

Zach. His name had been Zach, like Garth's dad.

Garth opened the pocket watch and looked at the boy's face. Did his son resemble him? He didn't know, and maybe a single picture wasn't enough to tell. There might be others. Did he want to see them, or would it bring more pain? And had Maggie's emails ever hinted at her secret? He couldn't think of any hints, but he still had the emails somewhere among those he'd downloaded from his work account before retiring. Was it possible he'd missed a cry for help?

The vibrating of his phone pulled him back to the present. "Hey, Cora," he answered after checking the screen.

"Gar—Dad, we're back, just like we promised, but can I help her brush them? Please? It'll only be fifteen more minutes. And where are you anyway? We saw the Jeep, but you aren't there waiting for us."

"What, you think I'm going to stare at an empty field for an hour?"

"Forty minutes," Cora said. "This horse is a little bit of a wimp, even if she is a darling. Ingrid says I could work up to her brother's horse in a few weeks, if I had the chance."

They didn't have a few weeks, but Garth didn't want to ruin her day now by pointing that out. "That's fine. I'll be back soon."

"Thanks. You're the best!"

He wasn't, and like most children who flung out such casual pronouncements, Cora didn't mean it, but the words somehow made him feel better. Garth came to his feet. He'd better get back there. He had a great sense of direction, but the sky was darkening, and he didn't want to get turned around.

He'd only taken a few steps when he stopped, thinking of Maggie. She was familiar with the area, but what if something happened to her? What if a snake bit her or she tripped over something and broke a limb? Whatever had happened between them, he couldn't leave her behind, any more than he could leave one of his buddies behind on a mission.

Wanting to be sure to mark his bearings, he pinpointed the direction where the remaining slice of sun was dipping behind the horizon. *It won't be long before dark falls,* he thought, hurrying in the direction Maggie had disappeared. Within a minute, the gurgle of water pulled him forward, and when he found the river, he walked along it. After another two minutes, he stopped when he heard shouting—not angry shouting, but voices tinted with laughter.

He moved again more slowly through the trees bordering the river, catching his breath when he saw her. Maggie was in the bend of the river floating on her back, her arms outstretched, her face heavenward. Except the hint of white in the murky water, her body was completely submerged, as if she were part of the nature that engulfed her.

For a stark, lonely moment, he knew he should be in the water with Maggie. He should be floating next to her, splashing her, and taking her into his arms for a passionate kiss. They had done as much in Trenton eighteen years ago when she'd teased him into the water at the riverfront. At the time, it had seemed a natural progression of their fascination with each other, one he desperately wanted to replay now. Maybe if they hadn't argued, they would have ended up here together.

Did that mean he wished she'd kept the secret? Had she been right in her decision at the base?

Revulsion washed through him. He dragged his gaze away and stared at the tree he was holding onto, barely resisting the urge to slam his fists into the rough bark. He'd come here to discover the truth, but this truth was one he couldn't bear. Yet it made a strange kind of sense—the baby explained everything that happened between them.

He heard voices again and looked to see Maggie swimming

to the bank after another woman he vaguely recognized from the café. Disconcerted, he turned and left them. Maggie was safe with a friend, and his sense of duty was fulfilled. She didn't need him.

Exactly as she hadn't eighteen years ago. Pushing the bitter thought away, he hurried back through the trees. More than ever, he yearned for someone to tell about his son, but the intimacy prevented him. He still didn't know where to go from here.

When he arrived at the corral, he saw no sign of Cora, and he assumed she was in the barn. The sun was gone, but the sky was still light, as if the world were suddenly on hold. He made his way across a field toward the Jeep he'd parked on the gravel road in front of the ranch house. Bringing out his phone to pass the time, he saw Ivy had sent him several new texts about Cora. Rather than answer them, he gave her a call.

"Hey," he said.

"Why isn't she answering me? Is she okay?"

"She's been with a girl here, riding a horse. They're brushing the horses now, so I'll have her call you when she's done."

"She's avoiding me."

"No doubt, but she has been busy today."

Silence fell between them, and then Ivy said, "What's wrong? You sound depressed. Is having a rebellious teenager there already dragging you down?"

He didn't miss the mockery in her jab. "It's not Cora," he said quietly, leaning back against the door of the Jeep. "I'm enjoying her, actually. But I'd be lying if I didn't say it felt like someone has taken away my little girl and given me back a grown-up stranger."

Ivy's snort showed zero sympathy. "I feel that way too, and I haven't been away from her. Mostly I'm glad to see her becoming an adult, but it's been hard this past year with everything that's been going on with her da—with Robert."

"She can't go back to that school," he said. "You see that, don't you?" Silence followed, and he couldn't tell if it was hostile or not.

Finally, she said, "I know. She told me she'd rather die, and I believe her. Even if it's mostly drama, I can't take the chance. But I'm not willing to let her go to Robert and that woman, or to her old school. Or to Florida."

"I know. We'll figure something else out."

"Yeah, but it's got to be fast. She can't miss her senior year. That would ruin her chances for college. You have to understand—I really thought a smaller town would be better for her. I honestly did. I didn't know it was going to be a school run by the stereotypical mean girl's mother."

"Bad luck, I guess." It was a lame thing to say, but Garth was still reeling from the knowledge Maggie had laid in his lap.

More silence, and then Ivy said, "What are you really doing in Forgotten? Cora said you were visiting a woman friend. She says you have an old photo of her in your wallet."

"I do, and yes, she is a woman." Last year when going through old boxes during Cora's visit, he'd stumbled on two photos from that day in Trenton. Unable to throw them away, he'd put them in his wallet along with three of Cora. He doubted Cora remembered them from a year ago, but she might have looked through his few pictures up in their room at the Butter Cake.

"Well, whatever you're there for, it doesn't seem to be working out for you. You sound miserable. Why don't you come here with Cora? You can sleep on the couch and help me figure this out. If you're still willing." It was an invitation he would have jumped at even a few days earlier.

"I do want to help, but I can't leave yet."

"Does that mean you're serious about this woman? Who is she anyway?"

Garth stared at the thin layer of gravel over the dirt on the road. "I can't leave yet because I just found out I fathered a son."

"What? You're kidding. When? How old is he?" Her voice rose with each short utterance.

Garth realized he'd have to tell her everything now, but maybe that was okay. He and Ivy had been close friends once, as well as lovers, and she knew him. Now that it wasn't Cora they were fighting about, she might be able to give him some insight.

"He would have been a little older than Cora. But he died of leukemia when he was a child. His mother was someone I knew before I met you, and she never told me about him. Well, she tried when he got sick, but . . ."

"You mean the woman singer who came to the base in Texas. She's the friend you're there to see?"

He was stunned at her comment. "Yes."

"I knew it! I would have had to be blind and deaf to not see there was something between you."

He pushed from the side of the Jeep and began pacing. "I swear to you that I never—"

"I know. You're not that kind of man." She sighed. "Anyway, I'm not complaining. You were better after that. More dedicated to us."

At least she'd recognized his effort. "Then what happened between us?" he asked.

For a long while, she didn't answer, but he could hear her tapping with her fingers—something she'd always done when she was nervous. "Besides the fact that you were always gone, and I didn't want to go overseas, well, I wanted another child."

"I know that. I agreed to adoption, didn't I?"

"I wanted my own child, to feel the baby growing inside me. I know I should have told you, but we were starting to fight so much, and it made me sound . . . like a witch."

The revelation didn't hurt—he'd suspected all along that his inability to father a child had been a wedge between them. His long absences certainly hadn't helped. "I suppose there are worse reasons for breaking up," he said. "But you never had another child. Why not?"

"About a year after I married Robert, I went to the doctor for some pain and other issues. Turns out, I had endometriosis, and it was a miracle I even had Cora. I had surgery, took drugs, but I finally had a hysterectomy last year. If I had gone in for the issues I was having during my marriage to you, it might have turned out differently. It wasn't you, after all. It was my problem."

Her problem. Was it possible he could father another child, that the baby with Maggie hadn't been a fluke? A feeling spread through him, but he couldn't identify what it was. He still felt numb with shock. "I'm sorry," he managed.

"I wouldn't blame you for pointing out the irony."

He sighed. "That wouldn't do either of us any good." He'd paced all the way back to the corral. Still no sign of Cora.

"Just so you know," Ivy said. "It hasn't been easy."

"Right. Not for either of us."

A pause, and then she asked, "So how do you feel about this woman now?"

"Her name's Maggie. Well, she was going by GiGi Blay when you met her."

"Right, I remember now. She had a beautiful voice."

Soft, silky, like the touch of a woman's hand. "Yeah. Anyway, she owns a bed and breakfast café here in Forgotten where I'm staying. And I don't know how I feel about her. That was the reason I—never mind that. The point is, she lied to me." So had Ivy, but he no longer loved Ivy, so that didn't matter.

"And you think things would have ended up differently if she hadn't?" Ivy asked. "What would you have done from Afghanistan?"

"I don't know. Something." He leaned back against the log fence of the corral, one heel lifted onto the horizontal log at the bottom. "A son, Ivy. I had a son. Do you know what that knowledge is doing to me?"

"If you'd known, you might not have married me."

That was true, and if he hadn't married Ivy, he would never have been Cora's father, even for those nine years, because he would have done anything to get back to Maggie and his child. Maybe he wouldn't have lost her.

"And if she told you at the base that day?" Ivy went on. "Then what? I don't know that I could have kept the secret if I'd been in her place."

"I don't know." It was impossible to say how knowing would have affected their future. On one hand, it might have broken them up. On the other, Ivy might have realized their infertility was her problem and they might have conceived.

"Okay, that's fair. But how do you know the boy was even your son?"

Garth's breath caught in his chest as he ran back over Maggie's words in his mind. Her words, her expression, her tears. He believed her. "I just do," he told Ivy.

Voices were coming from the barn now, and he turned to see Cora and Ingrid emerging with a gangly older youth in a lettered jacket, whose red hair hinted that he was Ingrid's brother.

"Hey, Cora's finished," he said. "I've got to go."

"Okay. If you ever need to talk, I'm here."

"Thank you."

"Make sure that girl calls me."

"I will."

Garth hung up without further comment. The relief of telling someone had lessened his anger, but he already regretted telling Ivy. He couldn't trust her with his heart.

"Dad!" Cora ran to him. "It was so great," she gushed. Looking around, she added, "Where's Maggie? I wanted to thank her."

"She had something she needed to do." Garth's stomach clenched at the partial untruth.

"I guess I can tell her later. But can I go riding tomorrow morning before Ingrid goes to school? She has to work tomorrow night till nine at the café, so she can't do it after. And can we go Saturday morning too? Please?" She clasped her hands together, looking more like the chubby eleven-year-old he remembered instead of the teen she was now.

"Yes," he said. "Sure. But Saturday is when I have to start getting you back to your mother." It would be at least an eight-hour drive, though he could probably stick her on an airplane in Lincoln or Topeka, if he wasn't ready to leave.

But why wouldn't he be ready? Walking away and putting all this behind him was probably the best decision he could make. Maggie had felt that way all along, after all. Still, he couldn't put it from his mind that he might want to leave now only to hurt her as she'd hurt him. Or would he be doing her a favor?

"I can pick her up at the Butter Cake," said the red-haired boy with a smile at Cora.

"That'd be awesome." Cora returned his smile with a wide one of her own. Obviously, the horse wasn't the only thrilling thing she'd discovered here. Garth tried to stifle his concern. It wasn't as if Cora would become serious about this boy or anyone in a day or two. Besides, they were both so young.

Cora's only a year younger than Maggie when I met her that day in Trenton, came the thought, startling him with the similarities. A single day. A young couple soon going their separate ways.

"I can drop her off," Garth said.

"Whatever." Cora gave a slight roll of her eyes.

Ingrid grinned. "I'm so glad you came. Make sure you come to the café tomorrow after school too. I'll tell everyone to be there to meet you."

Cora laughed. "Even the mean girls?"

"There's only a few snotty ones, and really, they can't be all that snotty or they have to go spend the day with Mayor Campbell. He's the best. Just stay clear of his wife." Ingrid made a face.

"I'll try to remember that." Cora gave a little wave as she started back to the Jeep with Garth. "I think Cora's brother likes me," she whispered, glancing behind her at the Patterson kids, who were heading in the direction of their ranch house. "He's so cute too. That red hair—he's like a Scottish Highlander or something. Ingrid says it's not fair she got all the freckles." She laughed and looked ahead at the Jeep, "Oh, there's Maggie. I've got to tell her about tomorrow." To Garth's utter surprise, she hurried forward to where Maggie was waiting for them.

Cora's story spilled out, and Maggie responded appropriately, but her eyes went past Cora to Garth, as if pinning him into place. Her loose hair was obviously wet, and her plaid blouse was slightly wet at the bra line.

"I'm glad you had a great time," Maggie told Cora.

Cora reached for the rear passenger door of the Jeep. "You gotta tell me everything you know about Ingrid's brother. He's so cute. Does he have a girlfriend?"

"Cora," Garth said in warning. "Remember, you're going home on Saturday."

Cora's shoulders slumped. "Don't remind me. Do you think if I begged, Mom would give me another week? What if I got sick?" She smiled hopefully at him.

Maggie laughed. "Thom's a good kid. A really good kid, actually. He used to work for me until he got a job at the turkey factory. And I don't believe he has a girlfriend at the moment."

"Cool." Cora opened the Jeep door but paused before ducking inside. "Wait, is your hair wet? Did you run into a sprinkler or something?"

Garth saw a flashback of Maggie floating in the river. "That's what I would like to know," he said, pushing the image away.

Maggie shrugged. "There's a swimming hole near here. We went on a walk, and I couldn't resist." Her chin lifted slightly as if challenging him to refute her statement.

He wanted to ask where her friend had gone and why she'd come back after their argument, but he couldn't do either without letting Maggie know he'd seen her in the water. If he admitted to an argument, Cora would question him relentlessly tonight. He'd probably have to tell her about his son too, but not now. Not until he knew more himself.

"Geez, Dad." Cora rolled her eyes at him. "And you wouldn't get in with her? Get a life." To Maggie, she said, "Do you think Ingrid would take me there on Saturday after we go riding?"

"I'm sure she would. If it's okay with Garth."

"It is, right, Dad?" With a pointed smile, Cora fished in her pocket for her phone and slid inside the Jeep, slamming the door.

That left Garth and Maggie alone. He knew he should get inside, but his limbs wouldn't obey.

"I'm sorry," Maggie said, her face calm and regally beautiful.

Her smooth voice slid over him like a sheet of the softest silk. "I know it's not what you expected. None of it. But I'm glad I could finally tell you. I'd like to tell you more about Zach and show you his pictures. I even have some video. You deserve to know—if you'd like to."

His eyes followed the curve of her cheek, the shape of her lips, the eyes that made him feel as if he were the only person in the world. "I don't know," he managed finally. More than anything, he wanted to learn about his son, but at the same time he didn't want to fuel the anger coursing through him since he'd learned the truth. He didn't want to hate her more.

"I understand." Her eyes didn't waver from his. "Let me know if you change your mind."

He drew out the watch from the pocket of his jeans and extended it to her on his open palm, but she closed his hand over it, her fingers comforting him with their heat. "It's always been yours," she said. "I was just keeping it for you."

Was this a preface to their final farewell? He didn't know how to feel about it, but he hated that he had to fight the urge to step toward her and take her in his arms—holding her was never going to happen now. He'd been wrong in coming here.

She started around the Jeep. "Come on," she called. "Let's go back to the café. Everything's closed on Main Street by now, but I'll make some fries for you and Cora. Kids always want fries."

Her movement freed him, and he opened his own door, pocketing the watch once more. His father would be so happy to see it back in the family. Of course, he'd have to remove the picture because he didn't want them to know about Zach. They'd suffered enough heartache losing Cora after the divorce.

He was all the way back to the café before he realized the irony. Maggie hadn't told him about Zach at the base when she'd come to sing because she hadn't wanted to ruin the life he'd made without her. Now he wanted to protect his parents in a similar manner.

It's not the same thing, he thought.

But maybe it was.

CHAPTER 17

On Friday, Maggie didn't see Garth or Cora all morning. They didn't come down for their free breakfast, and it was only seeing his rental Jeep outside the café shortly before lunch that she knew he was even still in town.

She'd blown it with him, but try as she might, she didn't see any other way she could have handled the situation, short of going back and changing the past, which was impossible. After thinking about it all morning, she placed her album of Zach in a cloth bag with a note and hung it on his doorknob. She could have another copy printed, if she had to, and having it might help Garth come to terms with the truth.

Or make him hate her more.

She went back downstairs and was swept up in the lunch rush. Keisha had altered her schedule to come in early that morning, so at least they were ahead. Even so, Maggie was happy when Charlotte showed up to help. "I've rescheduled my appointments for the next few weeks," she said, "so I can help during your rush times. Or until you find someone."

Maggie started to protest, but Charlotte held up her hand. "It's okay. I can use the extra cash. One of my ladies decided to go with a doctor at the hospital."

Maggie didn't buy it for a minute. Charlotte often had to turn women away from her services and sometimes traveled over an hour to other small towns to give prenatal care to her clients. But Maggie was grateful nonetheless. "Thank you," she said simply. Charlotte couldn't make the bread, but her help with everything else would be invaluable.

"How did it go last night after you went back to Ingrid's place?" Charlotte asked her when they were alone in the kitchen.

"He barely looked at me, and I haven't seen him yet today. So not good."

"He's probably thinking things through."

Maggie nodded but was glad when Keisha came for another order, cutting their conversation short.

Charlotte wasn't the only one who came to save Maggie from drowning. Hannah herself appeared at three when the rush was over and began tying on an apron.

"What are you doing?" Maggie asked her. "I told you not to come in after school."

"Keisha tells me you're having problems finding someone to fill my spot, so I'll come in a couple days a week and put in a batch of bread. It'll only take a couple hours, and I love doing it."

"I'm sure you have better things to do," Maggie said halfheartedly, looking around the kitchen that probably wouldn't pass any health inspection at the moment, though Charlotte was making headway on the dishes Keisha was bringing in from the tables.

"Not really. Besides, I miss you guys. And Dylan's working. In fact, he's out on an emergency call and probably will be gone the rest of today, so I'm all yours. Why don't you take a break right now? If I know you, you've already been here ten hours straight, and more than that yesterday."

Maggie fought tears as she hugged Hannah. "Thank you. I guess I do feel a little frazzled."

Hannah grinned and leaned closer. "You got friends, girl. Never forget. You helped me when I needed it most." She paused for a moment before rushing on, "But what is going on with that Air Force pilot? Keisha is very closed-mouthed about it all, except to say that he's here because of the video I made of you singing. Then today his daughter came to my class with Ingrid. She says you're old friends with him, but her tone seemed to hint you were more than friends. Is that why he's in town?"

"Wait, Cora went to school with Ingrid?" Maggie asked. "Is that even allowed?"

"Yeah, it is. The school encourages visitors, especially if they think they might enroll. We can use all the money we get for each student."

"I don't think there's any chance of that happening," Maggie murmured.

"I wouldn't be too sure," Hannah said. "I saw the way her father looked at you at the birthday party the other night—and the way you looked at him. What's going on?"

Maggie caught Charlotte's sympathetic gaze over Hannah's shoulder. "We dated once," she said. "A long time ago. But I don't want to make a big deal out of it."

"I knew it!" Hannah said.

Keisha paused on her way out of the kitchen and hooked her

arm through Maggie's. "Come on. Sit at the counter. You haven't eaten anything yet."

Relieved at the rescue, Maggie let herself be led away to the other side of the counter for the second time in as many days. She was eating a late lunch when a group of kids came in from the school, talking and laughing as they ordered drinks and food and pushed together a couple of tables in one of the corners. Cora and Ingrid were with them, and Maggie was happy to see Cora looking so content.

But where was Garth? She was tempted to go upstairs and see if the album was gone. Maybe it was better not to know. In fact, she should get in her car and drive over to Ronica's to see if she had any extra eggs she was willing to part with. A little time away would do her good. Maybe she'd even go out to the lake and doze in the afternoon sun.

Maggie's thoughts were distracted by someone sitting on the stool beside her. She turned to see a full-figured woman with short blond hair and a soft, friendly-looking face.

"Hi," Maggie said, habit taking over. The woman's face was vaguely familiar, but she wasn't a regular here.

"Hello." The woman looked up at the menu. "It all looks so good. What do you recommend?"

"If you don't have a favorite sandwich, you could get the soup and bread. It's all good."

"What are you having?"

Maggie had to look at her half-eaten sandwich to remember. "Turkey club with a side salad."

"I'll have that then. I like turkey." The woman gave the order to Keisha, who appeared like magic in front of them. Maggie felt a little silly watching without helping. If she was taking a break, she really needed to get out of here.

"Main Street here is so picturesque," the woman said. "Like a postcard. Really amazing."

She was definitely not from Forgotten. "Are you visiting?" Maggie asked, peering harder at her.

The woman nodded. "I have family staying here." She looked around the café, her gaze pausing on the group of teens. "Oh." The word escaped her mouth like a soft breath. "My daughter's over there."

Maggie personally knew all the kids' parents—except Cora's. "You must be Ivy," she guessed. "Cora's mom."

"Yeah." Ivy's attention returned to Maggie. "You look familiar. Have we met?"

"I'm Maggie Tremblay. I own the Butter Cake."

Ivy blinked several times and then nodded. "Aw, so that means you're also GiGi Blay. We met at the base in Texas—a boatload of years ago."

"We did." What did you say to the ex-wife of a man you'd loved and never gotten over? Maggie couldn't help the swell of envy in her breast. This woman had had more of Garth than she'd ever had.

Ivy smiled and put out her hand. "Nice to meet you again. Garth told me how kind you've been to Cora. Thank you for that."

Cora, yes. The teen was a safe subject. "She's a good kid," Maggie said. "She helped me here in the café yesterday morning. Very capable."

"That's what they say at the Subway where she works. Or worked, I guess. I think she quit when she . . . uh . . . before she came here." Ivy sighed. "Is Garth around?"

"I haven't seen him today, and I only saw Cora just now when she came in. Apparently, she went to school today with Ingrid. Ingrid's the one with the red hair and freckles. She works here."

"The girl with the horses."

"Yes."

Ivy smiled as Keisha slid a plate in front of her. "Cora has wanted a horse her entire life."

"Didn't we all? When I first came here, I owned a horse for a few years but ended up giving her to a farmer's daughter who rode her more than I did."

Ivy laughed. "Things change."

"Right." Maggie swallowed hard and glanced down at her plate. She needed to extricate herself before the pain of the meeting overwhelmed her. Instead, she asked, "You've come to take Cora home?"

Ivy's gaze once again went to her daughter. "I haven't seen her this happy for a long time. She's gotten to an age—well, let's just say it's been hard these past few years. I got divorced from her father last month—her biological father, I mean—and I thought moving from St. Louis would help, but it only made things worse."

"I'm sorry."

"We'll work things out. That's why I'm here. I couldn't wait for her to come home, especially when she keeps telling me she'll just run away again. So, I took the day off work, flew into Lincoln this morning, then drove here. I trust Garth, but I had to see for myself that she's okay."

"That's understandable. I'd probably do the same thing." It would have been easier if Maggie could have found a reason to dislike Ivy, but her dedication to her daughter was a plus in her favor.

"I'm not sure what I'm going to do." Ivy's eyes returned to Maggie's. "Her old school isn't an option, even if I trusted her to live with her father and his new girlfriend, which I don't. The crowd she was with was headed toward trouble."

"Garth seems pretty good with her."

Ivy bristled. "I'm not giving up custody."

"That's not what I meant. Maybe he has some ideas is all I was thinking."

"Sorry," Ivy said with a sigh. "I sounded more angry than I meant to. None of this is Garth's fault, and the fact that he's willing to help when he really doesn't have to says what a good man he is. I once thought keeping him from Cora would help her bond with her birth father, but all it did was keep her from having one more person around to love her. He was always more of a father to Cora than her birth father." Ivy swallowed, shaking her head. "The worst decision I ever made was ending our marriage."

So Ivy had regrets too, something they had in common. Did working things out mean she wanted Garth back in her life again as well as in Cora's?

"That's the problem with a lot of decisions," Maggie said. "There's no delete key."

Ivy snorted, and her blue eyes glinted with enjoyment. "You got that right." After a moment of silence, she asked, "Do you have a room available tonight? Well, and maybe tomorrow night. My plane leaves early Sunday morning. I have to be back for work on Monday."

"Sure," Maggie said. "I can even make up the trundle bed in the room if you'd like to have Cora move over to it with you. The bathroom is shared by one other room, but that one won't be occupied until Sunday, so it'll be private."

"Sounds perfect." Ivy touched Maggie's forearm hesitantly, her voice lowering. "Look, Garth told me about your son. I'm sorry—for both of you."

The words hit Maggie like a blow. Garth had told Ivy about

Zach? Why did that feel like a betrayal? All Maggie could do in response was to nod when she wanted to rip her hand away and run upstairs to grab Zach's photo album so she wouldn't have to share any more of her son with this stranger—or anyone else.

Ivy moved her hand, picking up her sandwich and putting it down again without taking a bite. "I . . . I feel I should say thank you. I know Garth is really upset, which is probably the only reason he told me, but after hearing what you did that day—or didn't do, rather—I want you to know how grateful I am. There was always a part of him I felt he withheld from me, but after that day, I didn't see it anymore. It might be selfish to say, but I'm grateful you didn't upset our lives when we'd just begun, especially for Cora's sake. She needed him, and so did I."

Maggie forced a smile, still too wounded to speak. Garth had told his ex-wife about their son. Had he also told Cora? Who else would he tell? Would all of Forgotten soon be asking her about it? After so long of not speaking about her loss, having the knowledge out there felt like a fire burning out of control. For so long Zach had been her secret, hers only, but now he was also Garth's to do with as he pleased, and that would take getting used to.

Oblivious to her inner dilemma, Ivy stood and waved at the teens. "Cora! Come here for a minute."

Cora's face went still. "Mom?" She jumped to her feet and rushed over. "What are you doing here?" There was no welcome in the girl's words. "I thought I had until tomorrow. You promised! Garth said I could hang out with everyone here until dinner today, and then he's taking me to the movies."

"Easy. Of course you can still do all that." Ivy held out her arms. "Come on. Give me a hug. I've missed you so much, sweetie. The past few days have been awful for me."

Fleeting guilt passed over Cora's features. "Sorry, Mom." She hugged her mother. "I couldn't go back to school, not after what happened."

"I know that now, and I'm sorry for not understanding." The two hugged again, with Cora looking more relaxed. "Where's Garth anyway?" Ivy asked as they pulled apart.

"Fishing, I think."

"Fishing?" Ivy made a face. "Since when?"

Cora shrugged. "I don't know. That's what he was planning when I went to school with my friend Ingrid. He was going to buy some gear and go. He's supposed to be back soon, I think. We're meeting for dinner at five and then going to a movie while Ingrid is working."

"Sounds fun. You can still do all that. My plane doesn't leave until Sunday. So, how was school?" Ivy's question was tentative.

"Great. It's really different here. Everyone's so nice."

"Honey, not everyone in Missouri is terrible. You loved your old school, remember?"

"Yeah, but you hated my friends." Cora's chin lifted in challenge.

"For good reason," Ivy countered.

Obviously, it was an argument they'd had numerous times— one they didn't need an intruder to witness. Appetite gone, Maggie pushed her plate across the counter where Keisha would take care of it and stood to leave. But before she could excuse herself, the front door to the café burst open to reveal a harried-looking Ronica Wilson.

"Is Fletcher here?" Ronica's frantic eyes scanned the few occupied tables. "Please tell me he's here." A complete and utter silence fell over the café.

Maggie hurried to her side. "I'm sorry, he's not. I haven't seen him at all."

Ronica's gaze latched onto Maggie's face as if thrown a lifeline. "He's missing. I thought maybe he might come here because it's familiar."

"What happened?" Maggie asked.

"Oh, it was so stupid—I was so stupid." Ronica twisted her hands together. "We had an early lunch, and he was talking to me as lucid as can be. Then he headed into the bedroom for his nap, like he always does, and I went to grab some lettuce from the garden to make a salad for dinner later. Then I did a few other chores inside the house while I watched a little TV. But when I went in to peek at Fletcher, to see if he was waking up, he wasn't there. I've spent the last hour looking everywhere on our farm for him. I called Jeremy in from the fields, and he realized the truck was gone. Fletcher must have found where I was hiding the keys."

Ingrid and the other teens gathered around them with concerned expressions. "We'll find him!" Ingrid said.

"Yeah, we can all look," added her brother. The other teens murmured in agreement.

"Thank you," Ronica said. "I'm about at my wit's end. Jeremy is out driving around our farm, and I called the chief on my way here, so he's getting his officers to look, but Fletcher could be anywhere. I can't believe this is happening." She began to cry.

Maggie put her arms around Ronica. "We'll find him." Lifting her voice, Maggie called out, "Keisha, Charlotte, contact the Ladies Auxiliary to get the calling chain started. Everyone who can has to get searching. We'll need to coordinate with the police."

"I'll pull up a map and start making assignments." Keisha reached under the counter for a tablet as Charlotte started calling. "Let's parcel it out." Customers in the café converged on the counter to get their assignments, led by the eager teens.

"What if he drives to Panna Creek?" Ronica asked as Maggie led her to an empty table near the door. "What if he runs over someone when he forgets how to drive again?"

"He'll probably stay close to what he knows. Was there anything you were talking about before he left?"

Ronica's face wrinkled. "I can't think of anything. But I can barely think at all. Oh, this is all my fault. I shouldn't have left him alone."

"We'll find him," Maggie repeated.

Ivy emerged from the group at the counter with her plate in one hand and her drink in the other. Maggie had forgotten all about her. Cora went with her mother to a table but quickly returned to the excited teens at the counter.

"Stay here," Maggie told Ronica. "I'll bring you a drink."

"Water, please. I'm too wound up for anything else."

"Okay. I'll be right back." Maggie looked at Ivy, who was calmly eating her sandwich, her attention still riveted on her daughter. Would they call Garth? And where was he anyway?

CHAPTER 18

Shortly after lunch, Garth headed to the Forgotten Reservoir with his new fishing gear in the back of his rented Jeep. He'd contacted the number on the property with the intact cabin he'd seen earlier, asking the owners if he could use the dock for fishing, and they'd been only too glad to oblige. Apparently, they had moved to Topeka and so far hadn't received much interest from potential buyers, though Garth suspected that might change once the pasta factory brought new residents to town.

He felt a little dishonest asking for the favor because as much as the place appealed to him, with the way things stood between him and Maggie, he wasn't a potential client. Staying in Forgotten was only an option if Maggie was part of his life, and now all those hopes had gone up in smoke. Besides, there was Cora now, and he'd likely have to rent something in another school district near Ivy's house to help her out.

Did that mean he was choosing Cora over Maggie? The

thought made his heart ache. Her secret had widened the gulf between them. How had it come to this?

He glanced at the passenger seat where he'd set the cloth bag holding the picture album he'd found on his door after buying the fishing gear. One glance inside had both chilled and pulled at him. Scores of photographs with decorations and comments—a definite labor of love—printed profession-ally. Did she think sharing their son's life with him would calm his anger? He'd been tempted to put the bag back on Maggie's door, but he couldn't. He'd already been cut out of his son's life. He wanted what was inside.

Just not at the café.

He turned right at the fork when he reached the lake and was nearing the sale property when he saw a silver truck abandoned almost in the middle of the road. He'd seen the truck before, hadn't he? Yes, it belonged to Ronica Wilson, the lady who'd brought Maggie milk and eggs for the café, the one whose husband was ill. The driver's door was open, but no one was inside.

Garth edged his Jeep slowly up to it and got out to investi-gate. The keys were still in the ignition. Leaving them there, he shut the door and drove around the truck, the tires of the Jeep going off the pavement into the dirt. Whoever had left the truck would probably be back soon. Maybe people always left their keys in their cars in Forgotten.

A little further on, he saw an old man walking down the side of the road, carrying a fishing pole, a white bucket, and a tackle box. His shock of white hair and his thinness in the brown plaid shirt and jeans made him easily recognizable—this was the old man he'd taken the hot coffee from at the café, Fletcher Wilson, Ronica's husband. But surely he hadn't been driving the aban-doned truck.

THIS FEELING FOR YOU

Garth drove past him, pulling into the sale property, and jumped from the Jeep. He met the old man in a few strides, angling into his path. "Hey," Garth said. "How are you?"

The old man stopped walking, his grin wide. "I'm good, sir. I'm going fishing."

"Oh, yeah? Does your wife know you're here?"

The smile widened. "Wife? I'm not old enough to have a wife." He looked around. "I thought the water was around here somewhere. Do you know where it is? I'm going fishing."

"Sure, I plan to do a little fishing myself. First time in about thirty years. Actually, more like the first time ever. I don't think I can count the time when I was a kid." Garth held out his hand. "I'm Garth. What's your name?"

"Name?" Fletcher's brow creased anxiously. "Where's the water? I'm going fishing."

Garth doubted Fletcher was supposed to be here on his own. How had he driven the truck? Or was his wife around somewhere? He could at least calm the man down before he figured out what to do.

"Come on," he said. "I'll show you where the water is, and maybe you can show me how to put bait on the line." He'd read articles this morning on his phone while waiting for Cora to get back from her early morning ride, but doing it himself might not be as easy as it looked on the video. He was almost glad Cora had abandoned him to visit the school and hang out with her new friends, so he could practice without her laughing at him.

He led the old man down the dirt drive, stopping briefly at the log cabin. The appeal was still as strong as the day before, and he wished he'd taken the owner's offer to go inside to look around. "Were you ever friends with the people who own this place?" he asked Fletcher.

The old man rubbed his chin, which wasn't shaved today, though Garth was certain it had been the other time they'd met. "Nope. Can't say that I do. Wait, is this your cabin?"

"No. I wish."

"Oh." Fletcher looked around vacantly before focusing on the fishing pole in his hand, as if discovering an old friend. "I'm going fishing."

"Well, come on then."

The brush had overgrown any path that might have once been here, but they made their way down to the log dock that had been built parallel to the water. Though they had to step over a section of mud to get to it, the dock was sturdy. As their feet hit the dock, a turtle that had been sunning itself near the edge dropped into the water with a soft *plop*.

The old man immediately fell to stringing something on his line and tossing it into the turquoise water with smooth motions that hinted at years of practice. Garth laid his new tackle box on the ground and took three times as long to put on his bait. Casting proved to be even more challenging.

"You're releasing too late," Fletcher said, coming around behind him. "Here, let me show you. When I say let go, let go."

Garth felt a little ridiculous. He was at least a head taller than the old man, who looked too frail to help anyone, but his grip on Garth's arm was like a metal wrench.

"Okay," Fletcher said. "Swing on the side. You can learn to do it over your head later. On three. Swing, swing, swing—release!" Garth did so, and the hook went flying.

"Oh, I see," he said. It was just a matter of coordination and timing, both of which he'd excelled at in the Air Force.

"Now you need to reel it in slowly. Or not. Sometimes if there's enough fish, you just need to wait." Fletcher chuckled and rocked back on his heels. "I caught the biggest fish around here. It's a town record, and I got the picture to prove it."

"Yeah? When was that?"

"Um. Last year, I think. The same year my grandma won the Planting Dance pie-eating contest, whenever that was."

Not last year, Garth decided, as the old man's grandmother had to be years in the grave.

Fletcher sat stiffly on the dock, his legs crossed like a young boy's. "Hmm." The old man set down his rod and gazed absently out over the lake.

Garth reeled in his line and then cast again. After six tries, he attempted a longer throw and was surprised at how far it went. *Not bad at all.* Almost immediately, he felt a tug on the line. "Hey, I got something."

"Huh?" Fletcher looked at him blankly.

"A fish."

"Oh, yeah. Well, reel 'er in." Still sitting, Fletcher grinned and grabbed his bucket, reaching into the lake to fill it with water. "Put him in here." He set the bucket on the dock, pushing it toward Garth. As Garth brought in the fish, Fletcher picked up his own rod. "Woah. I got one too," he called with a laugh. He jumped to his feet and began reeling in the fish.

"How do you get it off the hook?" Garth asked.

Fletcher hurried to show him. He might not remember his own name, but his body remembered fishing.

After bringing in two more fish over the next hour, Garth decided to call it quits. Cora would be back from school now, and he needed to clean up before meeting her for dinner. Returning to the café meant seeing Maggie—unless by some miracle Cora was upstairs instead of chatting in the café with her new best friend. Garth had so far managed to avoid running into Maggie by eating both breakfast and lunch out of the café, but at some point, he'd have to make a few decisions and stop avoiding her.

But what was he going to do about Fletcher? The old man was once again sitting on the edge of the dock, the legs of his jeans rolled up and his bare feet in the water. Garth couldn't leave him alone, so he'd have to take him back to Maggie's. "You ready to go?"

"Go where?" Fletcher leaned over and peered into the bucket where five fish swam around, bumping against the side of the bucket. That didn't include the three smaller fish they'd thrown back into the lake.

"You can have all the fish," Garth told him. "I don't have any place to cook mine. It should be plenty for you and your wife."

Fletcher looked blankly at him as if he didn't understand, then he slowly took a folded piece of paper from the pocket of his shirt and stared down at something written there. "Ronica," he murmured under his breath before putting it back into his pocket.

"Your wife, right?" Garth was keenly aware that something had changed in the old man.

Fletcher nodded and stood to cast out his line again, this time with an expertise that made his previous smooth attempts look clumsy. His face was somber, as if drinking in every movement and treasuring it.

"Are you okay?" Garth asked.

Instead of answering, Fletcher said, "This dock belongs to the Smiths, but they won't mind that we're here. They moved to Topeka several years ago to be near their daughter. They haven't been back since."

"You thinking of buying the place?"

"No. I already have a cabin." He pointed vaguely down the

bank to the right. "My kids say I should sell it, but I won't let them. Jeremy, at least, will want it once he has kids. The farm might be all he needs now, but kids love water. I did." He began reeling in his line.

Garth guessed the old man had been headed to his own property in the truck when his mind wandered. He'd been lucky he hadn't crashed. "Holding onto the cabin is smart," he agreed. "Besides, the land around here will be worth a lot more in a few decades, I'll bet."

Fletcher snorted. "I won't be around by then. At least I hope not. Ronica deserves better." He stared down into the water, and for a moment, Garth thought he was going to step off the dock and sink into the depths of the lake.

"Easy now," Garth said, wondering how deep it was here. They were near the shore, but he couldn't see the bottom on this side of the dock.

Fletcher met his gaze. "Don't worry. I'd never do that to Ronica or my children and grandchildren—when I'm lucid, that is. And when I'm not myself, well, I forget why it would be a good idea." He gave Garth a flat smile. "If I die when I'm not myself, be sure to tell everyone it was an accident."

That won't be today, Garth vowed. "How long have you been dealing with memory loss?"

For a moment, he didn't think Fletcher would answer—maybe he didn't even know the answer—but he finally said, "Ten years. That's when I was diagnosed. But it didn't get bad until a year or so back. I can't even understand the newspaper now . . . even when I'm all there. I still try, though." Fletcher stopped talking and cast his line again, a tragic, forlorn presence against the lush, verdant backdrop.

He obviously wasn't ready to leave, or maybe he thought they'd only recently arrived. Garth cast his own line again while he thought about what to do.

Minutes later, Fletcher glanced into the bucket, surprise on his face. "Wow, we've got so many! I can't wait to show my mom."

Garth stepped forward barely in time to save the man's fishing pole from the lake. He reeled in both poles and shut the tackle boxes. "Can you carry this?" he asked, handing Fletcher his box. "I'll give you a ride home."

"Aw, can I carry the fish instead?"

"Sure. Better get on your shoes first." He had been tempted to dump the rest of the water and the fish back into the lake, but he didn't want to mar the old man's happiness, however fleeting.

After donning scuffed work shoes, Fletcher picked up the bucket, his hands shaking as he tried to balance it. Garth moved forward to help, only to have half the bucket of water poured down his front.

"Oh, sorry," Fletcher murmured.

"Not a problem." Garth pulled off his T-shirt and began mopping his chest and pants. At least most of the water had poured to the sides, so he didn't look like he'd wet his pants— he hoped. "We didn't lose the fish—that's the important thing," he said as Fletcher's face drooped in a frown. "We would have needed to dump some of the water before putting the bucket in the car anyway."

Making sure the old man had control of the significantly lightened bucket, Garth balanced everything else and urged Fletcher up to the Jeep. There, Fletcher hopped into the passenger side while Garth put the equipment and fish in the back. He laid his shirt over his tackle box to dry. What to do with the old man now? No one had appeared to notice he was missing, but someone had to be worried. He should have called Maggie when he first found Fletcher and not let his ego get in the way.

He climbed into the Jeep with the old man. "Do you know where you live?"

Fletcher looked at him blankly. "Who are you?"

"I'm helping you take your fish home, remember?"

"What fish?" Fletcher eyed him suspiciously.

Garth reached over and pulled out the piece of paper from Fletcher's pocket.

"What's that?" Fletcher asked. "Is that mine?"

Garth opened the page and read:

Your name is Fletcher Wilson. Ronica Wilson is your wife. Be kind to her. You have Alzheimer's, which means you can't remember. If you can still read this, don't be a jerk. She is the most wonderful woman in the world. Don't forget! And to anyone else who might be reading this, if I can't tell you who I am or where I need to go, please call my wife.

A carefully printed phone number was at the bottom of the note.

"Wait here," Garth said as he exited the Jeep to make the call. The man might not know who he was at the moment, but that didn't mean he had to talk about him right in front of him.

"Hello?" came a breathless voice on the other end of the line. "Who is this?"

"Garth Dalton. Is this Ronica Wilson?"

"Yes."

"Good. I'm the pilot staying at the Butter Cake Café. I think we met the other day? Anyway, I'm at Forgotten Reservoir with your husband. I found him on the road with a fishing pole, so we've been fishing. I didn't want to leave him here. Is there someplace I should take him?"

"It's Fletcher!" Ronica screamed, nearly deafening him. "That pilot found him. They've been fishing!"

Garth held the phone away from his ear as more exclamations and questions came in a hurry. When the sound died a little, he put it back to his ear. "Yes, he's fine. He did leave your truck in the middle of the road. The keys are still in it, but I don't think he should drive."

"No. Of course not. Please make sure he doesn't get the keys. Where are you?"

"On the cabin road near the reservoir."

"Oh, thank you, thank you, thank you!" Ronica gushed. "Please, stay with him. I'll be right there."

"Sure, not a problem. Or I can bring him to you."

"I'll need to get the truck anyway. I'll have someone drive me."

"Okay, I'll meet you at the truck. We're further down at the Smith's cabin right now."

Back inside the Jeep, Garth froze as he saw Fletcher thumbing through Maggie's photo album, a gentle smile on the aged face. "That's Jeremy," Fletcher said, holding the book out to Garth. "Want to see?"

The page was open to Zach's birth. Maggie was holding him with an expression of complete contentment. She looked incredibly young, and she had been—only eighteen when she'd stepped into the same path that had captured her mother. The picture was followed by one of Maggie and another woman, who was crying as she rocked little Zach. A short description below made his heart ache.

I gave you life, my precious son, but your new mommy and

daddy will give you the home that I can't. It rips my heart in shreds and makes me wonder how I can go on, but I do this because you deserve everything a child should have, including both parents. You don't deserve a life on the road, seedy hotels, or irregular meals. You don't deserve to be neglected by a mother who can barely take care of herself or to crave the love of a man who is too far away to be your father. Oh, little one, I love you more than the earth or the moon or the stars. I love you more than breath or life. I love you forever and ever and ever. Please understand that this is the only thing I have left to give you now. But I will never be far should you ever need me again. Love, MT

Maggie had been only a year older than Cora was now when she'd become pregnant. He would hate the idea of Cora enduring what Maggie had endured. Garth had been four years older, and he should have been the one to step up and take care of Maggie that day, no matter how utterly, compellingly infatuated he'd been. But he hadn't, and she'd done what she'd had to do—given Zach the childhood she'd always wanted.

The pages that followed were full of proof that Zach's life had been good. There were pony rides and barbecues and days on the water. There were swings and friends and laughter. A man who carried him on his shoulders and helped him fish, a woman who lay with him on the grass while they made dandelion chains. Tidbits of writing explained each event, carefully marked with a date. There were also more pictures of Maggie with Zach, and each of these was followed by a longer text entry, but after the first one, which expressed a mixture of sorrow and joy at her longing for him, he didn't read those anymore. They were too private and personal, things Maggie should only tell him in person, if at all.

Then came the illness, the pictures in bed at home and the hospital. Each depicted a brave, smiling little boy, red-eyed parents, and also Maggie, whose suffering face and weight loss were dramatic, though her bright smile never faltered. He understood at once that she had been as brave as the child. Tears pricked his eyes, and he pinched his lips tight to stave off the emotion.

Beside him, Fletcher patted his arm. "I blew it with the first three kids," he said. "I was always out working, and I was too hard on them. Too impatient and strict. With Jeremy, it was different. I took him with me, I praised him, I let him have fun, I took time off. It's never too late. Remember that. My son loves farming, and he won't abandon his mother when I'm gone. You need to forget the bad and go on. Things change, and that's okay as long as you never give up."

Garth nodded, unable to respond aloud. He didn't know what year the old man was remembering, but a profound truth resonated in his words. Garth's eyes went back to the book, and he mentally traced each line in his son's small face. Even if Maggie had told him about Zach, Garth couldn't have been able to give more than Maggie and this couple had given his son because he wouldn't have guessed what was coming. He would have stayed in Afghanistan and accepted more assignments, believing they had a lifetime ahead of them. That was also truth, and Garth wouldn't hide from it.

"Thank you," Garth said.

The old man didn't appear to hear. He was already climbing out of the truck and waving at a bright blue compact car driving up behind them. The silver truck was behind the car, and Garth felt a twinge of guilt that he'd been so caught up in the photo album he hadn't noticed the passage of time. He put the album on the seat, blotted his eyes with his fingers, and climbed out of the Jeep, feeling a little awkward without his shirt.

Instead of the stranger he'd expected to have driven Ronica here, Maggie emerged from the blue car. She must have come straight from the café because she was still wearing her white blouse over a mid-thigh pair of yellow shorts that would have matched her apron, if she'd been wearing one. Her ebony hair was wound up on her head in several twists, and it glistened in the sunlight. Her creamy white neck beckoned to him.

"Thank you so much," she said to Garth as he approached, her gaze briefly grazing the scar on his chest before lifting to his face. "We were worried when we saw you weren't at the truck, but I figured you had all the fishing gear to put away."

Garth glanced over to where Ronica was hugging Fletcher near the side of Maggie's car. "We did get some fish. The guy has talent, even when he can't remember his name."

"I'm sure he loved that," Maggie said.

"He did."

"But you . . . are you okay?" Maggie's question came softly. "You seem a little . . ." She shrugged and trailed off, probably deciding he was still angry at her. But he wasn't, or at least not like he had been yesterday. He was angrier at himself. Everything about what happened was hard but hating—blaming her—wasn't going to fix the past. It also wouldn't take away his yearning to hold her, and both of these things were the reason for the moisture still gathering in his eyes.

"I'm fine," he lied. "I'd better get his stuff." He thumbed over his shoulder while backing away, his attention riveted on her. Swallowing hard, he turned and opened the back of the Jeep and removed the bucket and Fletcher's fishing gear. He was grateful for the moments to compose himself.

When he returned to Maggie, Ronica and Fletcher had joined her. "Thank you so much for looking out for him," Ronica said. "I was frantic when I found he'd gone. We were close to having the entire town out looking for him when you called."

Fletcher reached out for his tackle box. "I'm sorry, sweetie," he said. "I wish I could tell you what happened, but I . . . you know."

"I know." Ronica grabbed his face, pulling his forehead down to hers. "I should have remembered we were talking about fishing. I'm just glad you're safe."

Fletcher stroked her cheek. "You're too good to me."

"No." She reached for the bucket Garth had extended to them. "I'm a little hard to live with, I know. Come on. Let's go fry up these fish. I bet you'd like that, right?"

"I think I would. But you'll probably have to clean them." Fletcher gave a sad sort of laugh. "Since you don't let me use knives anymore."

"That's because you nearly cut off your finger. But I don't mind. Jeremy might even join us."

Ronica hugged Maggie. "Thanks for everything."

"Any time," Maggie said as they started to turn away.

"Wait, your pole." Garth held it out.

"Thanks," Fletcher said. "Have we met, young man?"

"I'm Garth. I'm staying at the Butter Cake."

"That's my favorite place to eat breakfast," Fletcher said. "Only don't tell my wife."

They all laughed, but the hopelessness of the old man's situation was a shadow looming over the couple. Ronica and Fletcher couldn't change the past or the future that awaited them. The fact that Garth had at least some choices left wasn't lost on him.

Garth and Maggie watched the silver truck drive away, the

silence between them becoming thick and awkward. "I'd better text Cora," Garth said. "She'll be wondering where I am."

"Actually, she knows. Ronica was at the café when you called. We were sending out search parties, and Cora was going to be part of that." Maggie paused a second and added, "So was Ivy."

"Ivy?"

"You didn't know she was coming?"

He sighed. "No, but I'm not surprised. She doesn't like to be away from Cora, and now that Cora has threatened to run away again, she's worried."

"When I left the café, Cora was ordering more fries," Maggie said. "She's waiting for you—they're both waiting for you."

That was his signal to bug out and close the metaphorical door between them. He could leave, knowing that nothing he could have written to Maggie in an email would have changed things.

He'd also know it was still as much his fault as it was hers.

"Can we talk?" he asked. The words felt like ash in his mouth, dry and chalky.

Maggie blinked slowly, her dark lashes leaving shadows on her cheeks. "I don't know if we should. You have a chance now to get your family back."

"What?" He stared. "No. No way. That's not going to happen."

"Why not? I think Ivy would be open to it."

He made the decision instantly, or maybe he'd done so last night when he'd watched Maggie floating in the water. Stepping forward, he closed the gap between them and reached for her hands with both of his. "Because I'm still in love with you, Maggie Tremblay. I've always been in love with you. I won't let the past decide the future. This time, I'm not walking away."

Her lips parted without sound. She stared at him for several long seconds before saying faintly, "But . . . Zach."

He nodded. "I know, and it's a huge thing for me to come to terms with, but I can do it. I know what you must have sacrificed for him to have a good life, and I want you to tell me about him. I want to know everything."

"But Cora and Ivy—"

"Will be just fine without me tonight." Releasing one of her hands, he took out his phone. "Cora would prefer to go to the movie with her friends anyway. She was taking pity on me because she wants to go riding again and to the swimming hole with them tomorrow."

"Okay," she said so faintly he had to strain to hear the words. "Let's talk."

He sent the text before pulling her in the direction of the Jeep, where he retrieved the photo album. "Uh, maybe we should go back to the café," he said. "There's no place here except one of our cars or the dock."

"I know a place. Come on." She took the book from him with a reverence he shared and began walking over the dirt drive in the direction of the cabin. When they neared it, she said, "Why are you here anyway? I mean, the Smiths won't mind, but there are plenty of public places to fish on the other side of the lake, though I suppose it's good that you were here—for Fletcher's sake, I mean."

"I'm here because of that." He pointed at the *For Sale* sign back at the entrance to the drive.

She stopped in front of the steps. "You're looking to buy?"

His resolve hardened. "Yes. And this is the place I want."

Shaking her head and grinning, Maggie bent over and took something out from a narrow opening under the porch stair. He was stunned to see a key. "Then it's just as well that we're here so you can take a look inside."

"And how did you know that was there?" He followed her up the stairs.

"Everyone knows. Well, at least the entire Ladies Auxiliary and everyone who works at City Hall. We take turns looking after the house for Beth Smith. You know, empty the mouse traps, make sure the pipes don't freeze in the winter, wipe up the dust, and check that vagrants haven't broken in. That sort of thing."

"Okay then." He watched her open the door.

The single floor cabin had only one bedroom, a small kitchen, and one bathroom, but the main room was large and comfortable, with a classic brick fireplace as the focal point. The only furniture in the entire cabin was a huge log bedframe in the bedroom that looked far too large to get out the door and a worn leather couch in front of the fireplace.

"They left a lot of dishes and utensils too," Maggie said, going to the leather couch. "We put in a batch of cookies when they have someone coming to look at it." She frowned. "That hasn't been for a while, but I'm assuming things will pick up when the pasta factory opens."

"I'm sure it will." The place was small, but the bones were good, and the new owner could always extend the bedroom and kitchen and add wifi. The fishing was a definite plus.

Maggie opened the book on her lap to the first page, but it wasn't one he'd seen before, so he must have started a page or two in. "This is me the week before Zach was born. He came a month early."

She was standing on the riverfront in a blue dress with her hand below her stomach that was poking out in a way that made his heart ache. She'd carried his child in her womb, her stomach and breasts had swollen with life, while he'd been fighting a war on foreign soil. He'd been dropping bombs on an elusive enemy, fighting to stay alive, while she'd been fighting an entirely different war. Two completely different experiences that perhaps neither of them could make the other understand. But they could try.

"And that's the adoptive mother?" he asked, pointing at the woman standing next to her.

She nodded. "Delitra. She looked after me when I was a kid. She was never able to have children, and when I realized . . ." She stopped talking, her lips pursing as she struggled for control. "I realized she would be the only one I could trust to . . . love him."

They continued turning pages, with Maggie sharing the stories behind the pictures. Not just the stories about Zach, but about her own life on the road as a performer. So much he'd missed and would have loved to be a part of.

One thing led to another, and before he knew it, he was telling her about his time in Afghanistan, especially the first years of intense loneliness.

"No wonder you got married the minute you were back in the States," she said.

"I missed you."

"I missed you too." She hesitated and then reached out to his bare chest, her hand lightly touching the white of his scar. "This looks like it was bad. What happened?"

"It was on a mission two years ago. I had to make a crash landing, but we all made it out safely. We even delivered our supplies, rescued a few people, and stole a plane." He held in a tremor as her hand traced down the scar, leaving an aching need in its wake.

"I'm sorry," she said, taking her hand away. "Forgive me. I shouldn't have—you must hate people staring at it."

He laughed. "It used to bother me, but not anymore—or at

least not much. It's a part of me. I have another impressive scar on my knee and a third, not-so-impressive one on the back of my head." He reached up to feel the raised spot. "Although that one was partially my fault for zigging when I should have zagged."

Her eyes dropped to the book with a sad smile. "I know about that. I've done my own share of zigging, though my scars aren't visible. So many mistakes."

He put a hand on her wrist, laying the other on one of the pictures. "If anyone is to blame for what happened back then, it was me. If Zach hadn't . . . come along, things would have been different. For you, and maybe for both of us."

"Yes." She lifted her gaze, sparking a hunger inside that shocked him with its intensity. "But you have to understand. I wouldn't change it. I mean, I wish Zach had lived, and I wish things had been different so we could know him now. But he was perfect, and I will *never* regret having him." She paused, swallowed hard, and added, "Even though it cost me . . . so much."

Her words made a strange kind of sense. He felt similarly about the crash that had nearly taken his life. If he hadn't been on that plane and had not forced himself to finish the mission, more soldiers would have died. He wouldn't take his choice back, not to save himself the months of pain or the scars on his body. Her scars were every bit as real and much deeper. He had no doubt about that.

"I think I understand," he said. "And it's okay now."

She smiled, her face a light in the darkness of his soul. "For what it's worth, if things had been different, I would have never broken up with you after our emails."

"And I would have come back. I promise you."

"I know that now." But her hand pulled out from under his. "I'm glad you finally know about Zach."

Panic started in his heart at the finality of her words, at how she seemed to be physically distancing herself—or getting ready to. Was he losing her all over again? "I meant what I said, Maggie. I have never stopped loving you, and I believe we can start again."

Her eyes studied his, seemingly at a loss. "How? How can we possibly get past this?"

He didn't really know, but he'd do everything in his power to try. "We start with forgiving," he said. "I forgive you. Do you forgive me?"

"Yes, but you don't owe me anything," she said.

"It's nothing like that," he began. What he wanted for her—for them both—was more, so much more, and suddenly he knew what he had to do. What he *wanted* to do. He was no longer the young pilot who craved dangerous adventure, a man who had fearlessly—even recklessly—risked his life for God and country, but he needed that man now, the same man who had allowed himself to fall completely in love in a single, blissful day.

He slid from the couch to his knees in front of Maggie, reaching into his pocket for the only thing of value he had there: the pocket watch. He'd used it in Trenton, and it was time to try again.

"This feeling for you still takes me by surprise, Maggie Tremblay," he said. "As if there's no beginning and no end. It's still just you and me. Will you do me the honor of becoming my wife?"

Her eyes widened, and a faint breath escaped her lips. The merest breath and nothing more.

"Well?" He waited for an answer, his insides so twisted, he could barely breathe.

If she said no this time, it would be over for good. If she wanted him to leave, he would respect her wish. No matter what lies she

had told, his actions had already hurt her enough. She deserved happiness, even if she had to find it without him.

Maggie loved telling Garth about their son. She appreciated his questions, his insight, and his eagerness. She ached for the sadness she knew he felt at not having been there, but at some point, he'd come to understand that the girl she'd been had done everything she was capable of doing. That understanding was more than she deserved but far less than she hoped for.

Less, because the spark, that little something Ivy mentioned at the café, still lived inside Maggie, and even though Ivy thought it was gone from Garth's heart, the spark had endured long enough to bring him here. The spark had driven her to reach out and trace the thick scar slashing across his muscled chest and wish that she'd been there for him. And the same spark had ignited into a flame that demanded she never stop touching him.

Garth hadn't hidden anything from her in the end, and she'd been wrong about so many things. He'd become a hero and a good man, someone she was proud to have known and to share a son with. At least now they could both go forward, even if it meant saying goodbye. Maybe this time, without the secret of Zach between them, it wouldn't hurt so much.

Except before she could leave, Garth slipped from the couch and on to one knee and asked her to marry him.

The last time he'd asked her eighteen years ago in a motel room, she'd laughed at him, saying she was far too young to spend years waiting for a soldier, even a fancy pilot in the US Air Force. Her flippant response and later refusal to give him her contact information had hurt him, but he'd still insisted she take the watch at the waterfront when he'd promised to find her.

She hadn't believed him. She'd laughed and buried that perfect day in her heart, not knowing how deeply the regrets would later consume her.

Now, unbelievably, miraculously, impossibly, here he was again, asking the same question all these years later, using the same words that had inspired her famous song and offering her the pocket watch instead of a ring. She didn't know him, and yet she felt he was the only man she'd ever really known.

"It's a simple question, Maggie," he said, his voice low and sexy. His closeness was intoxicating, and she ached for his touch.

But he was wrong. This thing between them—their past, the spark, the hurdles they would have to face—wasn't simple, and she was old enough now to know that.

"I can't leave Forgotten," she said finally. "It's my home."

"I would never ask you to." He looked around. "I'll buy this place, and when I feel the need to get back to the skies, I can pick up commercial airline work in Lincoln or Topeka and still be here half the week. In the meantime, my half-pay retirement is plenty for a small town like this."

"What about Cora?"

He took her hand, rubbing his thumb across her palm in an achingly tender manner that made her crave more. "I don't know yet, but this isn't about Cora. It's about us. It's about us and our future children, because I want more children with you, Maggie, if you're willing. I won't abandon Cora, and I don't regret her any more than you regret Zach, but don't you think it's finally our time? The way it should have been after Trenton?"

The way it should have been. When she had been the laughing, talented young woman and him the eager, brilliant pilot. She reached out and put her free hand over the watch as she had all those years ago, but this time her response would be different—because she knew about regrets. She'd longed half her life for another chance, and it was finally here.

Her song played in her head. *Can I hold onto myself while reaching out for you?* Once, she hadn't thought that possible. Now she understood that saying yes might be an impossible leap of faith, but saying no was inconceivable.

"Yes, Garth Dalton, I will marry you." *I only want to be with you.*

He pressed the pocket watch into her hand as he moved forward to kiss her, pulling her closer. Their hearts beat together, the heat of his bare chest radiating through her as she responded to his kiss.

This feeling for you, her heart sang. She'd waited so long to feel this way about a man, never dreaming it would be the same man whose laugh and smile and touch had once changed her forever.

CHAPTER 19

*A*fter the breakfast rush died down Saturday morning, Maggie waited expectantly for Garth, Ivy, and Cora to come downstairs. Garth had been closeted in Ivy's room, hashing out an idea he and Maggie had brainstormed regarding his stepdaughter, while the teen slept unaware after a late movie with her new friends. Ivy showed no expression as she reached the counter, but Garth looked pleased with himself, which Maggie guessed meant Ivy had been receptive.

Cora, still unaware of their collusion, was in a hurry, anxious to go riding before her trip back to Missouri—or Misery, as she was calling it. "I'm not really hungry," she said to Ivy as Maggie ushered them into the kitchen for a private breakfast at the small table. "I need to go soon. And after we go riding, there's a swimming hole they want to show me. I might not be back until late."

"You have time to eat," Ivy said. "Besides, we have something to tell you."

"I can't leave yet. Please, Mom." Cora flounced into a chair, her face drawing into a pout.

"That's what we need to talk about," Ivy said, sitting next to her.

Maggie went to the stove to dish up their plates, and Garth came with her. She stepped closer to him instinctively, as if her body couldn't stand to be apart from his. They'd both had little sleep last night as they'd planned for their future with an urgency of those who had already lost too many years, but she felt wide awake. Everything around her looked new and precious, as if a curtain had been pulled from her eyes . . . and her heart.

"What if I just stayed here?" Cora shot into the abrupt silence. She picked up her fork as if ready to stab someone. "I bet Ingrid's family would let me stay with her, and I could come home on some weekends. Or maybe I could stay here with Maggie and work after school. I'm practically an adult, and you're not home from work when I get there anyway." Cora's gaze slid past her mother, her eyes pleading with Maggie and then with Garth. Something in one of their expressions must have consoled her because she relaxed her death grip on the fork.

Ivy laid a hand over her daughter's. "I've been talking with Garth, and I've decided you can stay here," she said, "but with Garth, not your friend. At least for the next school term."

"Really?" Cora stared at her mother, her eyes wide with disbelief. "I can stay? You really mean it?"

"Yes. We'll have to work out an agreement with the court giving Garth temporary guardianship so you can attend school here, but you'll have to agree to stick it out at least a term. I'll come visit on weekends, or you'll come visit me. In the meantime, I'll look for a new job closer so you can live with me and finish out the rest of the year here. Most likely, my job will be in Panna Creek, not Forgotten, but either way, we'll work out living arrangements and transportation, so you can still go to school here."

Cora launched herself at her mother. "Oh, thank you! I promise you won't regret it."

"There are conditions," Garth said, setting plates in front of Ivy and Cora. "You need to make this school work because your mom can't be jumping around jobs again to get you into another school district, and I'll be staying in Forgotten permanently. This morning, I made an offer on a cabin by the reservoir. It needs some work, though, so for now, we'll be staying here at the café."

"That's so cool!" Cora let go of her mother to pop up from the table and hug him as well. "Thank you! I'll make it work. I swear I won't be stupid again, and besides, the kids here are nicer."

"They won't be perfect," Garth warned.

Cora nodded and slid back into her chair. "I know. But no way can it be as bad as back home. I'll be good, I promise."

Maggie set down a plate for Garth opposite Cora and next to Ivy, but he grabbed her hand and didn't let go. "There's something else you need to know," he said. "Maggie and I are getting married."

Cora's hand stopped with her fork halfway to her lips. "Wow." She glanced at her mom, apparently searching her for signs of distress and finding none. "I thought maybe—" She shook her head. "Yeah, okay. Cool. Congratulations. When's the wedding?"

Maggie and Garth were married a week later in the church across the street. There were no bridesmaids or groomsmen, or fancy speeches, but Maggie's mother and stepfather were there, and Garth's family had flown in from Florida. Maggie was gratified by their enthusiastic acceptance and a little embarrassed when his father, Zach, became a little teary-eyed at the sight of the pocket watch. But when Garth made a show of kissing her after the ceremony, to cheers from the audience, Maggie had to blink back her own happy tears.

A reception followed in the City Park next to the Butter Cake Café, organized by Hannah Morgan and featuring a buffet prepared by the Ladies Auxiliary. Half the town showed up to wish them well, and the presents included boxes of fruit, vegetables, a side of beef, and cheeses.

Keisha, Charlotte, and Hannah would take care of the Butter Cake during her weeklong honeymoon in Trenton, where Maggie and Garth planned to retrace their first steps together. Cora had arranged to stay at Ingrid's for the week, with both of them and Lisa Whang working at the café after school and on Saturday. Even if things didn't go smoothly, Maggie knew the town wouldn't care in the short term. They were all too happy for her.

"Thank you so much," Maggie told Charlotte and Keisha as they came to wish her well.

"Are you kidding?" Charlotte said. "This makes me believe in miracles."

Keisha snorted, giving a toss of her dark hair. "I wouldn't go that far, but I'm excited for you. If anyone deserves a happy ending, it's you."

Maggie sensed a sadness behind the words—or maybe it was determination. The first thing she would do upon returning home would be to discuss what Keisha really wanted. She'd been hiding at the Butter Cake since her accident, but maybe it was time to help her move on. The first step was the most painful, as Maggie well knew.

"Well?" Hannah looked pointedly at Maggie. "It's time. Now or never. Are you ready?"

Maggie smiled back. "Yes."

"Okay then." Hannah hooked an arm through hers and led her up the gazebo steps. Maggie's hand locked onto Garth's and pulled him along.

"Hello, everyone," Hannah said into a microphone balanced on a thin metal stand she'd set up in the gazebo. "The bride and groom are about to take off in their fancy new Jeep that some of you have been kind enough to decorate so outrageously." Laughter ran through the crowd. "But before they do, Maggie is going to throw her bouquet and then perform a special song. Come on. All you single girls and women, please come over here in front of the steps."

Every eye went expectantly to Maggie, who promptly turned her back to the crowd and threw her bouquet. Screams rose as the single women scrambled for it. When Maggie rotated quickly to see the winner, Keisha blinked up at her, stunned. "Oh, no," she said flatly. "No freaking way. Not me." She threw the bouquet in her hands at a prepubescent teen who caught it and giggled with joy.

"Well, that was interesting," Hannah said over the laughter. "Congratulations! Now everyone, quiet down for 'This Feeling for You,' a song from our own Maggie Tremblay!"

Most of the town had heard before today that Maggie was also GiGi Blay, and if they hadn't, the appearance of her well-known former agent at the wedding had quickly settled the question. Axel Zyon was one of the few who knew the story behind the song's creation, and he made no secret about wanting to stage her comeback with a heartfelt story about her wedding to the man who had inspired her famous song, but

Maggie refused. Today was private. It was their day, hers and Garth's.

Even so, her soul *was* soaring as snippets of new songs filtered through her brain, begging to be set on paper. Perhaps someday she would release more songs, but only if she could do it from Forgotten because this was her home, and these people were her family. She loved her café and her life.

Grinning, Maggie turned to a tug of Garth's hand.

"I love you," he mouthed.

Her hand briefly went to the pocket watch around her neck, now finally in full view. Somehow, it perfectly set off the wedding dress that Natalie, the Police Chief's wife, had made this week. "Oh, yeah?" she challenged, exactly as she might have responded at eighteen when she'd been that sassy young girl at the waterfront. "Well, listen up, Mr. Dalton, because this is how I feel about you."

Smiling, she took the guitar leaning against the side of the gazebo and stood next to Garth as she sang her song into the microphone. There was a new verse now, a fourth one that had always been missing, though she'd been the only one to know. This was the song as it should have always been. Even the third verse that she'd written after placing Zach with Delitra took on a new meaning—because Garth had swept away her regrets, and with them all the sorrow and pain.

Maybe she'd meant the verse for him all along.

This feeling for you took me by surprise,
Makes me question who I am and who I want to be.
Your laugh, your smile, your touch have changed me.
That look in your eyes tells me you feel the same.

This feeling for you.
This feeling for you . . .

This feeling for you, helpless to ignore.
Can I hold onto myself while reaching out for you?
I look for your smile, ache for your touch.
No beginning no end; there's just you and me.

This feeling for you.
This feeling for you . . .

This feeling for you is all that I know.
Sorrow and regret and pain, you slip away from me.
And I only want to be with you.
This feeling is us—real and true and endless.

This feeling for you.
This feeling for you . . .

This feeling for you took me by surprise.
Your laugh, your smile, your touch, shows me all we
will become.
The past is new, the future ahead.
No beginning, no end; always you and me.

This feeling for you.
This feeling for you . . .

HISTORY OF FORGOTTEN

and James and Chelsea Morgan

In the late 1850s in Missouri, James Morgan, the son of a wealthy farmer, and Chelsea Fortson, the daughter of an important abolitionist cattle rancher, fell in love and wanted to marry, but their fathers were sworn enemies, divided on the issue of slavery, so they separated their children, forbidding them to associate or fall in love—as if such a thing could be mandated.

Not that their fathers didn't try. James was made to travel to Virginia, where his father, who had been elected to government office, moved in an attempt to influence the politicians there in favor of slavery. Chelsea was sent to what would eventually become Kansas to live with relatives, who, like Chelsea's father, were firmly on the side of Kansas entering the Union as a free state. For three years, James and Chelsea lived apart with nothing more than secret letters passed between them, aided by loyal friends and servants.

James worked hard managing one of his father's farms, and he eventually put together enough funds to get himself to Kansas to ask Chelsea to run away with him. He showed up on her door-step, his identity disguised, and she packed a bag and left with him that same night. When their marriage was discovered, both of them were disowned by their disgruntled families.

They thought that would be the end of their struggle, and their families would eventually come to accept their union. Unfortunately, they married in early 1861, near the same time Kansas was formed and became a free state. Embittered by his defeat, James's father considered his son's marriage an affront to his entire way of life, and it wasn't enough to simply disinherit James for his betrayal. Instead, he sent a posse after him, made up of the wildest, ferocious, and murderous men. They found James in Kansas and shot him. Chelsea, eight months pregnant with her first child, threw herself in front of him. Her beauty was such that these ruffians took pity on her and left him to bleed out in her arms.

Chelsea, accustomed to tending wounded cattle, stopped the bleeding and called for a doctor. James's leg had to be ampu-tated, and he nearly died of infection, but Chelsea slowly nursed him back to health, all the while keeping his survival a secret. She wrote to her father, begging for his help and forgiveness and telling him about his grandchild. Only years later did she learn that he'd died after being shot by his pro-slavery enemies. Her brother inherited their large ranch and, being a greedy man, tore up her letter so he wouldn't have to share.

When no help came, Chelsea earned a living making ravioli at a restaurant during the day and sewing dresses late into the night until James was finally well enough to come out of hiding. By then, they wanted nothing to do with their families, so they took off to the northern part of Kansas near the border of what would become Nebraska. They built a one-room cabin and began to farm. Thirteen children were born to them, and Chelsea often walked the fields at night with her children, hand-in-hand, teaching them the harvest songs.

When people passing through the area asked James and Chelsea where they were from, they claimed they'd been gone so long that they'd forgotten because they feared word might get back to their families. Most of the couple's thirteen children married people from nearby towns and returned to help farm the land. The town became known as Forgotten, a place of a new life for all those who had been or wanted to be forgotten, and where thirteen was the luckiest number.

To this day, weddings, birthdays, and other special events are always planned for the thirteenth. Every year in Forgotten, the town celebrates the first harvest by singing the harvest songs and reenacting the story of James and Chelsea Morgan with the hope that Chelsea will bless the harvest for another year.

Legend has it that people who stay in Forgotten, especially those running from their past or those who want to forget, usually end up finding themselves.

℘Rachel Branton has worked in publishing for over thirty years. She loves writing women's fiction and traveling, and she hopes to write and travel a lot more. As a mother of six great kids and with a growing number of grandchildren, it's not easy to find time to write, but the semi-ordered chaos of her life gives her a constant source of writing material. She's been known to wear pajamas all day when working on a deadline, and is often distracted enough to burn dinner—well, when she remembers to cook it. She lives in central Florida and loves going to the beach with her husband, hanging out with her grandchildren, and riding very tall rollercoasters.

Under the name Rachel Branton, she writes romance, romantic suspense, and women's fiction. Rachel also writes urban fantasy, paranormal romance, and science fiction under the name Teyla Branton. For more information or to sign up to hear about new releases, please visit www.RachelBranton.com.

www.ingramcontent.com/pod-product-compliance
Lightning Source LLC
Chambersburg PA
CBHW070918180626
46817CB00003B/1114